Appearances Too

A Novel

K. Reshay

ISBN: 1977710034

ISBN 13: 9781977710031

Acknowledgments

This has been one of the most exciting times in my life. I have been able to take words from the thoughts in my head and put them into a book. I have also been fortunate enough to have people read those words and actually enjoy them. It is a feeling like no other to have someone compliment and support you on your craft.

God, I thank you for my gift. I thank you for your grace and mercy that have guided me thus far. I thank you for determination and courage. I acknowledge and appreciate this blessing.

To my husband and my two boys, thanks for giving me time to focus on my dream. Thanks for every encouraging word, every hug, and every sacrifice you all have made so far. I love you.

To my parents, sister, grandpa, and in-laws, thanks for all you do. You all have truly encouraged me and allowed me to be myself. I truly appreciate the love and support.

To the rest of my family, thanks for being there. Thanks for every book you have sold for me. Thanks for every social media post and every book review, and above all else, thanks for the support.

To my best friend, thanks for all the years you've listened. You've always been there for me. You are truly my big sister.

Last but certainly not least, my readers. Thanks for taking time out of your life to allow me to introduce you to the ideas from my head. It was your encouragement that helped me fight through the late nights and thoughts of giving up. It was your encouragement that allowed me to continue to press forward.

Now grab your wine, light your candle, and get ready for *Appearances Too*.

Much love,

K. Reshay

Chapter One

Toni

I'm just a soul whose intentions are
good. Oh Lord, please don't let me be
misunderstood.

—The Animals, "Don't Let Me Be
Misunderstood"

Toni regretted seeing Laila the moment their eyes locked. She tried looking away quickly, but to no avail. It had been months since Ricky and Laila's divorce and she didn't know how to reach out to her. She swallowed and forced a smile. After ordering her coffee, she reluctantly obliged the situation.

"Hi, Laila!" said Toni as she walked over and gave her a hug.

"Hey, girl! How are you? What are you doing at the hospital?" asked Laila, hugging her back.

"Oh, I'm doing okay. I could be a lot better, though. I'm here with Ty. He was injured by someone trying to rob him," Toni said, sounding defeated.

"Oh my God, Toni! Is he okay?" asked Laila, visibly concerned.

"It's a long story. He's still not clear on what happened, but for the most part he's okay. I just came down here to clear my head a bit," Toni said.

Just then, the barista called both the ladies' names. They walked over, grabbed their cups of java, and sat down at Laila's table.

The Starbucks lobby in the hospital was so serene. There were people who were looking at their phones and laptops and reading. Everyone in the coffee shop was in their own world. Toni wanted to be one of those people. She wanted to disappear with her music, coffee, and thoughts.

The argument Toni just had with her husband Ty had brought up some old feelings Toni never really dealt with. She always felt inadequate. Even though Ty tried to act like he didn't understand, she knew he did. She couldn't help thinking how different her life would have been had she found her own man instead of stealing Ty from Maya.

"So what are you doing here?" Toni asked with hopes of not mentioning Ty again. She was still pissed off and didn't want it to spill out. She'd been married long enough to know that the last thing she needed to do was bad-mouth her husband to anyone. She felt like she had no one to talk to about Ty, anyway. Other than Maya, she really didn't have a lot of friends. Especially ones to talk to about her personal business.

She'd learned early on not to tell Maya any of her problems with Ty. Maya would just get quiet, anytime she would mention any discourse with Ty. It seemed like she was trying to fight the urge to say, "That's what you get." She never really offered any real advice either. Toni was always the listening ear and voice of reason for Maya's problems, though.

"Girl, I'm here with my sister, Joan. She's having baby number three. She doesn't live too far from here," said Laila in between sips.

"Oh, that's awesome! What is she having?" asked Toni, checking her phone for messages. She was trying desperately to sound interested in Laila's conversation. But she couldn't shake off the fact that she still hadn't heard from Ricky or Maya.

"Another boy. I tell you the truth—boys are going to be the death of us." Laila laughed.

Toni admired Laila's smile. She was stunning. Her hazel eyes, smooth chocolate skin, and long eyelashes always made her look as if she was wearing makeup. She had thick, curly hair that shaped her face in a neat fro. She was around five feet tall and had a slightly thick build.

"So how have you been doing?" Toni asked reluctantly.

Laila exhaled. "I've been making it, girl. I've relocated to Atlanta. It wasn't easy. I lived with my sister for a few weeks until I found a cute apartment off of Peachtree. I've also started working for CNN as a marketing executive. It's not as glamorous as it sounds, but it does pay the bills," Laila said as she sipped her coffee and glanced toward her newspaper.

"Laila, I'm so sorry to hear about you and Ricky. I've been meaning to call you, but you know how that goes," stated Toni, wanting to stop ignoring the elephant in the room.

"It's fine, and I really appreciate that. I'm not crazy, Toni. I realize that you have to divorce friends too, sometimes. It's a part of it. So how's my Jessica doing?" asked Laila. She knew there would be plenty of time to talk about Ricky's trifling ass soon enough.

Toni smiled. The mere thought of her little angel made her forget about any negativity. "She's good. She's growing up fast as a weed, very sassy, and definitely a daddy's girl." Toni pulled out her phone and showed Laila her recent pictures.

"Oh, Toni! She's a doll. I'm going to make sure I get back in town to see her after all of this is over," said Laila.

"That sounds like a plan. I could use the company." Toni smiled, unaware of the fact that she was forgetting to keep up *appearances*.

"Really? I would think you'd have your hands full dealing with Miss Shit Don't Stank! I mean Miss Maya and her wedding," Laila joked.

Toni felt disturbed by the mention of Maya's name. She shifted in her seat, rolled her eyes, and sucked her teeth before responding. "It definitely has been different," she said, trying not to roll her eyes again. Her body language had a way of expressing her true feelings.

Laila paused as she glanced at the newspaper again. She'd received an epiphany. *So that's why we didn't go to Maya's surprise engagement party. His sorry ass was fucking her fiancé. All that talk about how tired he was and Maya don't care for us no way shit was all bull*, she thought.

"Well, speaking of your girl Maya, here's her photo in the marriage section of today's paper. She must have taken out ads in every paper in the state!" Laila said as she pushed the paper toward Toni. She sat back with her coffee, smugly wanting to reveal the information she had. It never even occurred to her to even say anything about Ricky to his friends. It had taken a lot of counseling for her to realize that she wasn't the reason her husband had cheated, but no amount of counseling would let her mind comprehend why he cheated with a man.

Deep down, Laila had developed a seething hate for Ricky. She didn't want to go to his friends because she wasn't sure if they even knew. Friends will be around the lover and the spouse and still show every tooth in their mouths. She flashed a devilish smile.

Toni looked at the photo reluctantly. "Well, they certainly look good together. I know she's excited about her new beginning," Toni said, trying to sound like the supportive friend. She knew Laila didn't like Maya, so she had to still show some loyalty to her.

"Is that right? What do you know about Steven Sims?" Laila asked, leaning forward.

"Let's see. He's an accomplished attorney for Wilshire and Associates, and he treats Maya very well and seems like a pretty genuine guy. Not to mention, he's sexy as hell." Toni laughed. The laughter felt good. It was needed just as much as her caramel Frappuccino.

"Toni, I have something to tell you," Laila said, sitting straight up in her seat.

"Yeah, what's that?" asked Toni, reading the caption below her best friend's engagement photo.

"Accomplished attorney Steven Sims is the reason why Ricky and I divorced," Laila said.

Chapter Two

Ty

Detectives Price and Reed arrived back at the hospital. They'd reviewed the parking-lot cameras, but the security lights were blown, so the image was shaky at best. All they could make out was the vehicle pulling in and some tall figure getting out. The camera faced the back of the person's head, so there was nothing concrete.

Detective Reed made notations of Ricky's physical appearance. He felt like Ricky had something to do with Ty's attempted murder. It was all a matter of proving it, as far as he was concerned.

What he couldn't figure out was a motive. He checked Ricky's background and didn't see anything that would show ill intent toward his best friend. *It has to be something we are overlooking*, he thought.

Both detectives thought that Ty's time with his wife might jog his memory. They stood outside of his door to continue to compare notes.

Ty took a deep breath as the nurse checked his blood pressure. It hurt to inhale. He regretted the first breath after the throbbing commenced on his brain.

"Are you in pain, Mr. Weeks?" asked the nurse.

"Yes, extreme pain. My head is throbbing so badly," Ty said.

"Okay, I'll go and grab you something. I'll be right back," she stated as she fluffed his pillow.

Ty noticed that she wasn't as nice and friendly as Nurse Brown. She was very polite, but he could tell this was business as usual for her. He couldn't wait to get out of the hospital. The term *within the blink of an eye* hit home tremendously as he considered his current circumstance. He'd gone from healthy to hospitalized all in a matter of hours.

He closed his eyes and thought back to his argument with Toni as the throbbing in his head continued. In all of this time, he never considered Toni's feelings. He always thought that she was his first choice. Girlfriend and wife are two totally different things, he rationalized.

He knew that Toni would overcompensate at times. He wanted to believe it was due to her just wanting to be a good wife. Deep down, he knew it was because she saw how successful Maya was and didn't want him to wish he had chosen her.

He had to admit, Maya had come a long way. He admired how successful she'd become, but he hated how she shoved it in their faces every chance she got. Even though she was successful, she couldn't compare to Toni.

Toni had unlocked a sexual side to him he never knew he had. He'd never desired a woman as much as he did Toni. His mind drifted back to finals week of their junior year in college.

Everyone was cramming for their upcoming exams. The libraries were packed. He and Toni were going to meet at the Sunbeam Cafe near Five Points South in downtown Birmingham.

The cafe was the best place in town to get a mocha cappuccino. It became their meet-up spot while hiding their relationship from Maya. Its dimly lit interior and comfy sofas provided the perfect studying atmosphere. Most of the people who came to Sunbeam were folks either going to work or getting off work. College students would come by some, but not very often.

Ty ordered two mocha cappuccinos and waited for his lady. While waiting, he thumbed through his psychology notes. His mind wasn't on the notes, though. The steam from the cups reminded him of the steam from the shower the night before.

Toni had decided to take a shower after they'd finished studying. It was late, so she just decided to stay over. Ty waited until she was in about ten minutes before he walked inside. The water and bubbles cascading off of her body made Ty jealous. He quietly removed his clothes and joined her.

Her erect nipples invited his warm tongue to suck them. He raised Toni's right leg and began thrusting his nature inside of her walls, leaving no room for her to escape. She felt so good. It felt like her juices were wetter than the water. Her pussy curved to him like it was made specifically to satisfy his needs.

As his mind wandered about their freaky shower episode, in walked Toni. She was wearing a blue jean miniskirt and a light-pink tank top. She looked beautifully casual to him.

"Hey, babe, how are you?" he said as he stood to greet her. Ty could see that Toni noticed he wasn't the only thing standing.

"Hey, baby!" she said, trying not to blush. "I see you already placed our order. Thanks so much because I've been craving one of these all day," she said, taking a sip.

"Well, what I've been craving wasn't on the menu, but yeah, they are good," Ty said slowly, biting his bottom lip.

"Hmm, well, what have you been craving, Mr. Weeks?" Toni asked, playing along.

He leaned over and whispered in her ear, "I've been craving your sweet pussy, baby. I want to taste you."

"What about your psychology final? I thought you wanted me to help you study?" She smiled, trying to look innocent.

"Meet me in the restroom in five minutes," Ty said as he left the table. He looked back at her in hopes that she would oblige his request.

The restroom was located near the exit and entrance doors. He figured Toni could leave right after without the stares of wondering patrons.

With her pussy throbbing in anticipation of Ty's explosive sex game, Toni packed up his bag and sauntered into the men's restroom. Luckily, no one would be able to walk in because it was a single.

As soon as Toni walked in, they began to kiss passionately. Ty couldn't control himself. He loved everything about her. Her smells infused his nostrils. He inhaled her scent deeply. It drove him wild.

He pulled up her skirt and ripped off her pink-and-purple thong. He lifted her up on his shoulders and began twirling his tongue around the inside and outside of her pussy. Toni always made sure she was Brazilian waxed for him. She tasted so good. He lapped up every drop she gave him.

Toni pulled up her shirt and bra, exposing her perky breasts. They bounced up and down as she rode his face. She placed the bottom of her shirt in her mouth to mask her uncontrollable moans of ecstasy. Ty was softly moaning too. Each moan from him turned Toni on even more. There's nothing like the moan of a man, especially knowing it's you making him do it.

Her hands reached for something to hold on to, but it was no use. She had to grab his head to steady herself. He felt so good that she could barely contain herself.

Ty's dick was so hard that he had to feel Toni's insides or he would explode. He pulled it out, never stopping the tongue thrashing. Once it was exposed, he lifted her down and pushed inside. She was so wet that he glided in effortlessly.

Secretly, he wished he lived inside of her moist walls. He was home there. She grabbed the back of his neck and ran her fingers through his hair. When they became one, the passion was undeniable.

Ty admired how Toni took the dick. She didn't run from it, like Maya. He would have to chase her around the bed because she backed up every time he went deep. Ty called it the Scoot Back Game.

Toni wasn't scared, though. She threw her pussy back on him like his inches weren't shit. She rode him while he held her body against the wall. She twirled around on it and savored every minute of its pleasure. Within minutes, they both exploded onto each other.

Toni's silky cum saturated his dick. He didn't want to let her down, but he knew they had to get out of there. He was sure someone would be knocking soon, and he didn't want the embarrassment to hinder Toni's sexual courage in the future.

"Damn, baby, you felt so good," he said, letting her down.

"You felt so good. I have to get out of here and shower," she said in between breaths. She grabbed some paper towels and cleaned up while he stuck his head out the door and stuffed her torn thong in his pocket.

"Okay, the coast is clear. Go on, and I'll call you in a few, baby," he said.

"Sounds good! I hope I satisfied your craving," she said, kissing him and then exiting quickly.

Ty snapped back to the present as his new nurse entered the room. She apologized for the delay and gave him his medicine. He placed his hands over his erection, hoping she wouldn't notice.

"Now, Mr. Weeks, this dosage is a going to be a little bit stronger than before. It'll make you drowsy, but you'll feel a lot better," she stated while adding the medicine to his IV drip.

Once she left, Ty yawned and closed his eyes. He hoped that when he opened them, Toni's face would be the first thing he would see. He needed her more than she would ever comprehend.

Chapter Three

Ricky

These wounds won't seem to heal. This
pain is just too real. There's just too much
that time cannot erase.

—Evanescence, "My Immortal"

Ricky turned off his radio and forced himself to listen to the loud sounds of the thunder. Any other time, he would have postponed a drive during a storm like this, but not today. Today had been scarier than the storm.

Ty could remember everything at any time now. Ricky was like a sitting duck. He had to get to Steven to figure out their next move. While he didn't want his friend to be dead, now he wished he were. *If only Ty would have just stayed away, none of this would have ever happened*, he thought.

He didn't want to face the fact that he was to blame for getting caught. His brain forced him to blame Ty. What once was remorse was now rage. He loved his friend, but he hated him for finding out. He hated that he confronted him with his truth. The truth that cost him his marriage. All normalcy was out of the window for him now. Ty's death would have been more welcoming. A tear rolled down his face as he hung his head in his own shame and selfishness.

While looking for his phone, the sound of honking caused him to swerve. That along with his nervousness was too much for him to handle, so he pulled over on to the side of the road. There, he was alone and left to face his demons within the quiet confines of his car.

The storm outside represented his world. Lighting, thunder, and the fear of the unknown may prove to be too much to bare. He thought of pulling back on to the inter-state and driving backward, forcing a head-on collision. His truth was just that conflicting.

Suddenly, the sound of Luther Vandross's "If This World Were Mine" broke him out of his desperation. It was Steven's ring. He feared the voice on the other end. He answered.

"Hey, where are you?" Steven asked, sounding a bit concerned.

"I'm on my way. But, Steven, Ty's not dead," Ricky stated, sounding defeated.

"Tell me you're fucking joking! Where are you?" Steven asked.

"Why would I be joking about something like this? Two detectives just left my house and said that he was found last night. Did you even check his pulse to see if he was still alive? I told you we should have just called the police.

And, to make matters worse, he has short-term memory loss," explained Ricky.

"Where the fuck are you!" screamed Steven.

"I'm about forty-five minutes away," said Ricky, unsure of what to say next.

"Well, don't meet me at the restaurant. Meet me around the side of the Birmingham Jefferson Convention Center," stated Steven. And with that, Steven hung up.

Ricky slammed his phone down and sped ahead, secretly wishing he would lose control of his car and crash. He didn't want to admit it, but Steven intimidated him. Ty's attempted murder wasn't the first time he'd seen violent behavior from Steven. His mind went back to the Atlanta incident.

Last year, they decided to go to Atlanta to celebrate Steven's win against Don's Wholesale Corporation. That was one of his toughest cases in his career to date. After checking into the Hamilton, the two men headed to Marquette, a gay club in Atlanta.

The night was going fine. The music was on point, and so were the drinks. Ricky knew they had to drive back to the Hamilton, so he stopped on his second Ketel One martini.

Steven, on the other hand, was on drink four. The more he drank, the louder he got. Ricky had never seen Steven like this before. Disappointed in his lover, Ricky excused himself to the restroom. While there, he saw one of his college buddies, Darnell Pulaski.

"Darnell Pulaski, how the hell are you, man?" asked Ricky.

"Man, what's going on with you?" Darnell asked as the two lightly embraced.

"Well, it's been a long time. What are you doing here?" Ricky asked sarcastically.

"Hell, I should be asking you the same thing," Darnell said jokingly. "But no, I'm here with my sister, Jasmine. She's dating that blond bartender over there and asked me to meet her. She seems pretty cool. We're just here hanging out until she gets off, and then we'll head over to the Waffle House. What about you?" he asked.

"I'm hanging out with one of my buddies. He won this big case and knows one of the owners, so free drinks. I've never been to a place like this, but it's where he wanted to go," Ricky stated while shrugging.

Truth was, Darnell was lying just like his old college buddy. Neither guy was prepared to explain to the other that he was gay.

The guys continued their conversation for a few minutes, mostly laughing and reminiscing about old times. Quickly, Steven ran over and pushed Darnell into a wall. "Get the fuck out of his face!" Steven yelled.

Darnell punched Steven in the face. "Who the fuck are you, motherfucker? I'll kick yo'punk ass!" screamed Darnell.

Ricky grabbed Steven while a few other patrons grabbed Darnell.

"Who is he, huh? Who is that motherfucker?" Steven screamed at Ricky.

"He's my friend from college, Steven! Are you out of your fucking mind? What the hell is wrong with you?" Ricky yelled.

The two men tussled with each other until they made their way out of the club. A couple of bouncers helped them.

Once they were in Ricky's truck, the two men argued. Ricky was so embarrassed and upset. He almost wrecked pulling out of the parking lot.

"What the fuck was that? What was that? You're not my damn boss, Steven! Do you have any idea how embarrassing that was? Do you?" asked Ricky.

"I should be asking you that. Here I was waiting on you, and you're in some dude's face. How about introducing me?" Steven hollered.

Ricky pulled over at a nearby gas station. He turned to Steven.

"Have you lost your damn mind? I'm married, Steven. What the hell am I supposed to introduce you as? My fuck buddy?" asked Ricky, clearly ready to beat Steven's ass.

"Oh! Is that all I am to you, Ricky? Is it? You tell me right now, or I'll walk my ass back to the Hamilton!" Steven yelled.

Ricky wouldn't respond. He couldn't. His truth would have ruined his affair. Instead, he dropped his head, as if waving the white flag of surrender were too much.

Tears welled up in Steven's eyes, but he refused to allow them to fall. Ricky knew that Steven thought he meant more, much more than being reduced to only sex for Ricky. He decided not to get out of the truck. Ricky decided not to drive off either. The two men just sat there, unsure of tomorrow.

Damn, I should have just followed my first mind and left his crazy ass back then, thought Ricky.

Chapter Four

M a y a

*Tonight, I'll be your naughty girl. I'm callin'
all my girls. We're gonna turn this party
out. I know you want my body.*

—Beyonce, "Naughty Girl"

Maya danced around her condo, looking for the perfect outfit to wear on her date with Steven. She finally settled on a dark-pink dress by bebe. It accentuated her slim frame just enough to show what few curves she possessed.

Now, all I need are the right shoes, she thought as she settled on a pair of green stiletto pumps. She was in such a good mood. Seeing Toni's life crashing down all around her made Maya want to laugh.

"I love to love ya, baby. I love to love ya, baby!" she sang as she finished up the last bit of cleaning. The rainy day didn't seem as gloomy anymore.

She poured a glass of red wine, settled in on her plush white sofa, and watched the storm outside. The breeze from the open window screens made the flames of her

Peach Mango Salsa Yankee Candles dance. She checked her phone.

Hmm, no more missed calls or texts from Toni, she thought. She took another sip of wine and decided to give Toni a call. Her terrible mood and news would be the icing on the cake.

The phone rang and rang, but Toni didn't answer. She decided to leave a voice mail. "Oh my God, Toni! What is going on with Ty? I lost my phone but finally found it! Call me, girl. I'm praying for y'all," she said as she pressed the end button. Maya could hardly contain her laughter before hanging up.

She thought her laughter was well deserved considering all the tears she'd shed over the years. As the thunder clapped, her thoughts sauntered to the first time she saw Toni and Ty out together.

The movie *Brown Sugar* was set to hit theaters. She saw the previews and wanted to go. Her love life was in shambles. At that point, she hadn't dated apart from Ty. She texted Toni since they were on decent terms, but Toni didn't even bother to respond.

The day of the movie, Maya decided to just go by herself. She loved Taye Diggs and thought a nice romantic comedy would snap her out of her depression and help her believe in love again.

She took the time to curl her hair, but her makeup was minimal. She decided on a light jacket, the amber scarf Ty had bought her, and jeans.

She was in such a good mood. The weather was a bit cool, so she stuffed her favorite blanket in her bag. She also packed her bag with her favorite drink and snacks because no one pays twenty dollars for movie snacks. After double-checking to make sure she had everything, she was out the door.

She had purchased her ticket earlier that day, so she didn't have to wait in line. Although she was fine with going alone, she wasn't fine with standing in line with all of the couples. She didn't notice Ty and Toni at the concession stand. After settling at the top of the already-crowded theater, Maya was all prepared to watch the movie.

The remaining seats filled quickly. It was mostly groups of girls and couples. Maya couldn't help but feel the loneliness. Soon, the movie started, and Taye Diggs's beautiful smile more than made up for that feeling.

During the movie, she heard giggling a few rows down from her but didn't pay it any attention. It wasn't until the scene where Mos Def was trying to hit on Queen Latifah during the New Year's Eve party that she realized the giggle belonged to Toni.

She sat up and saw Toni lay her head on Ty. He leaned over and kissed her forehead. Maya sat back and was unable to finish chewing a mouthful of gummy bears. So they just dissolved.

The movie no longer mattered. Instead, Maya watched the new couple. They seemed so comfortable together. They laughed, hugged, and kissed throughout the movie.

Maya couldn't help thinking that she should have been in Toni's seat. She should have been on the receiving end of Ty's kisses. She should have been the recipient of Ty's love.

She moved her blanket up to her face to absorb her tears. She silently thanked God for the darkness. As hard as she tried, she couldn't look away from them.

Once the movie was over, Maya couldn't get up to leave. She kept her head down as if she were getting her things together. The movie patrons passed her, unaware of her extreme pain. When everyone was gone, she just sat there thinking of Ty and Toni. There in the empty theater, her sadness turned into anger. She removed her amber scarf and left it in her seat.

She hurried out of the theater, not even remembering the movie she'd just watched. All her thoughts were of Ty. She realized that she still loved this man. She'd always thought that he was the one. She couldn't even begin to rationalize what she'd just witnessed in the theater.

She wanted to find Ty and Toni. She wanted to yell at the top of her lungs at them. She wanted them to understand that it simply was not fair for their lives to carry on as if there were no pain left in the path. She wanted them to not be together.

That night, Maya cried. She shed tears for her dad. It had been years since his death but the pain seemed to remain. She also shed tears for her loss of love and friendship. The betrayal had proven to be too much. She wondered how the hell she would ever get through it all.

Maya took another sip of her wine as the memory began to fade. She felt as though her emotions never officially left that theater. The song changed on her Pandora station. "Who gave you permission to rearrange me? Certainly not me," sang Erykah Badu.

Good fucking question, she thought while gulping down the rest of her wine.

Chapter Five

Toni

After Laila's comment, Toni stopped midsip and looked at her with a puzzled expression. Ricky had told her and Ty that he and Laila split due to a number of reasons. The main reasons were her inability to handle her spending and their constant arguing. He said he was done once he checked their accounts and found all of them were overdrawn.

"What does Steven have to do with your divorce?" Toni asked, looking confused.

Just then, Laila's phone started ringing. It was her sister's husband. He told her the baby was on its way and her sister needed her.

"Oh God! That was my brother-n-law. He said that my sister is having the baby now and is asking for me. Look, Toni, I have to go, but I'll call you soon," Laila said, grabbing her things.

"Wait a minute, Laila! You can't just spring something like this on me," Toni stated.

"Just tell your best friend, if I can even call her that, to be careful. I'll call you." And with that, Laila hugged her and left.

Toni just stood there, confused. *What the hell does Steven have to do with their divorce*? she thought. Toni grabbed the newspaper and stared at Maya and Steven's picture. They looked so happy and sophisticated. She was in awe of the write-up. Her friend was so accomplished. She figured Steven must have given Ricky legal advice on their divorce or something.

Laila walked toward the elevator, feeling defeated. She knew she'd signed a gag order during the divorce. She didn't know what had come over her. She did hope that that little bug would at least raise some doubt on perfect Steven. She exhaled as she pressed the elevator button to her sister's floor and prayed Toni would not only remember what she'd said but relay the information to Maya.

Toni gathered her things, including the newspaper and left Starbucks. She found solace on the La-Z-Boy recliner near the windows overlooking the lake in the hospital lobby. She put in her ear buds and found the app for Pandora on her phone.

As the melody of Aaliyah's smooth vocals soothed her soul, she wondered about the past hours. So much had happened in so little time. From the impromptu trip with Maya searching for Steven, to the late-night call from the hospital about Ty, Toni's mind was in orbit.

She picked up the newspaper and looked at Maya's photo again. That wasn't the girl she'd met in college years ago. Her eyes were not the same. Toni dropped her head, knowing that she had contributed to that.

Maya never did anything to Toni before she stole Ty. Maya was always there for her, especially when she needed to go see her boyfriend in Biloxi. She felt responsible for Maya's behavior. There was no way to explain to herself why she fucked Ty, so she didn't even try.

She felt like she should just hash out shit with Maya once and for all. It had been years of appearances, and she was just ready to either work things out or move on with her life. She loved her best friend but knew deep down why Maya no longer was a friend to her.

She noticed her light blinking on her phone. It was a missed call from Maya. She cleared it out as Tyrese's "Sweet Lady" played. She wasn't ready to talk to Maya. She had to get things straight with Ty first. She loved her husband, but she couldn't help but regret her decision back then. Their one mistake has caused so much drama and pain. This realization made Toni question if Ty would have eventually left her alone if she'd never seduced him.

She closed her eyes and imagined life without him and Jessica. She couldn't do it but knew that Maya's life certainly would be different. Maya might not have been a housewife like her, but she certainly would have been happy. Maya loved Ty. She opened her eyes. The water in the lake didn't seem as relaxing anymore.

Sigh...

Chapter Six

Ty

"What's taking so long, huh? Where is my baby?" asked Ty's mom, Mildred.

"Mildred, he's hardly a baby. Ty is damn near forty years old, for heaven's sake," stated Ty's dad, Jerome.

She and her husband paced back and forth, waiting on the lady at Patient Services to find Ty's room number and get visitors' badges.

Mr. Weeks was a short, stocky man. He was dark skinned with a small fro that would put you in the mind of Fred from the sitcom "Sanford and Son." His teeth were all spaced apart, but his personality more than made up for his outward appearance.

Mrs. Weeks was a snooty lady that disliked Toni and loved Maya. She was around five feet five inches and very slender. Her skin was caramel. She wore her salt-and-pepper hair in a long bob style. Her standing appointment at the beauty salon ensured that it always looked flawless. She was an attractive lady.

They met Maya for the first time when Ty brought her home for Thanksgiving dinner. She and Maya hit it off instantly. Maya felt right at home. She helped prepare dinner and set the table and everything. Ty's mom admired the fact that she helped and didn't just sit in the front room.

Mildred had only met one other girlfriend of Ty's, so she knew Maya was special to him. The next morning, she and Maya went Black Friday shopping while the men went on their traditional hunting trip. She told her husband later that night how happy she was for her son. She and Maya spoke often on the phone after that.

Ty's parents came to Birmingham to celebrate New Year's Eve with them a few weeks later. There, they met Maya's best friend, Toni. Imagine Mildred's surprise when Ty showed up later with her instead of Maya. Mildred couldn't believe it.

Now this is one trifling heifer, Mildred thought as she shook Toni's hand, faking a half smile. Toni could sense Ty's mom was being fake. She was unsure if his mom would even remember meeting her. The way she turned her nose up at her gave her the answer.

Mildred ended up calling Maya after Ty and Toni left. She had to get to the bottom of what was going on. Of course, Maya laid it on pretty thick. She told Mildred how she loved and trusted Toni. She told her that she'd caught her and Ty together and that they ended up fighting.

Mildred apologized over and over to Maya. Maya cried her heart out over the phone to Mildred. She told her about her dad and how Ty was there for her and everything. Mildred couldn't believe how Ty let a sweet girl like that go.

Toni never really did anything to Mildred, but Mildred harbored a deep resentment there. She figured if Toni could sleep with her best friend's man, she was simply a woman that could not be trusted. She realized that with Toni, she could never let her guard down.

"Excuse me, sir, the badges are ready. You can go up now," stated the receptionist.

Ty's mom snatched them out of her hand and headed for the elevators.

"I apologize for her. She is just upset about our son," Ty's dad stated, walking backward.

The receptionist just nodded. She was about to get off and really didn't give a damn. All she knew was that she was off until next Friday, and the weed was already rolled up in her purse.

The detectives were waiting near Ty's door when they arrived. Detective Price nodded his head as Ty's parents walked by them. Ty was still asleep when they walked in the room. The nurse put her hand to her mouth and motioned for them to be quiet. Ty's mom gave her a mean look.

"Hi, I'm Jerome Weeks, and this is my wife, Mildred. We're his parents. Can you tell us how he is doing? What happened?"

The nurse told them as much as she knew. Mildred began sobbing quietly. "Where is Toni?" she asked in between sobs.

"I think she went downstairs. She's been gone a few minutes," stated the nurse.

"I'm not surprised. If Maya were here, I know she would never leave my baby's side," Mildred stated bluntly.

"Look, Mildred! Enough is enough. I am sick and tired of this shit now. Ty is a grown-ass man, and he made his decision. Toni is a nice daughter-in-law and does her best to take care of our son and granddaughter. Let it go, Mildred. It's been years now. Just let the shit go, please!" Jerome stated, clearly pissed off.

The nurse took this as her cue to leave. She knew that their argument might disturb Ty, but she wasn't as caring as Nurse Brown. She wasn't as concerned with his recovery.

"Let it go? I will never let it go. She should be ashamed of herself for stealing her best friend's man! Then, she *married* him. This stuff happening now is just the beginning. You reap what you sow," said Mildred, walking toward Ty.

Detectives Price and Reed overheard the argument. The fact that Toni had stolen Ty put things into a different prospective.

"This Maya person may have had a reason to hurt Ty. We need to get more background information on this Ty, Toni, and Maya situation," stated Detective Price. Detective Reed nodded as he wrote his notes. They stopped talking when Toni stepped off of the elevator.

"Mrs. Weeks, how are you doing today?" asked Detective Reed.

Toni exhaled. "As good as I can, Detective."

"We'd like to ask you a few more questions, if you don't mind," Detective Reed stated.

"*More questions?* Well, whatever you all need. I'm not sure if I know anything else," Toni stated.

"We'll be the judge of that," stated Detective Price, cutting off Toni. "Now earlier, you mentioned that you were out last night with Maya. Your best friend, right?"

"Right, and why are you asking me about that again?" asked Toni.

"We actually overheard her name again today. How is your relationship with your best friend?" asked Detective Reed, calmly walking over, trying to ease the tension created by his partner.

"Our relationship is fine. We are best friends, as I said before," said Toni.

"Well, *where* is she?" asked Detective Price.

"What do you mean?" asked Toni.

"I mean, she's your best friend, and your husband was found in the trunk of a *car* last night. He was robbed, beaten, and left for dead. What kind of best friend would not be here to support you?" asked Detective Price boldly.

"The kind who is busy planning her wedding. Besides, I haven't even talked to her. She doesn't even know yet," stated Toni, getting visibly upset. Both detectives noticed how her demeanor changed.

"I thought you were with her last night?" asked Detective Price.

"I *was* with her earlier last night, but I haven't talked to her since she dropped me off. The nurse called me early this morning," stated Toni.

"What's Maya's relationship with Ty?" asked Detective Price.

"They're friends, of course," stated Toni, getting agitated. She felt as if they were wasting too much time talking to her and not out looking for who had done this to her husband.

"Hmm, let me ask that again. What *was* Maya's relationship with Ty?" asked Detective Price.

Toni looked at each detective, confused. She didn't understand their line of questioning. Just then, Mildred walked out of Ty's room with the smuggest look on her face. Toni knew then why the detectives were questioning her about Maya. Common sense would say that leaving her would give Maya a motive to hurt Ty.

"Detectives, I don't understand what that has to do with anything, but if you must know, they used to date in college," stated Toni bluntly.

"And now you're married to him?" asked Price with a straight face.

"Yes, happily married," Toni said, not taking her eyes off of Mildred.

The detectives nodded at her and walked toward the elevator. Detective Reed knew that there was more to the story than what Toni was letting on.

"Oh, by the way, Mrs. Weeks. What's Maya's last name?" asked Detective Price.

"Fisher," answered both Mildred and Toni.

Chapter Seven

Ricky

Ricky saw Steven's car as soon as he turned the corner at Texas de Brazil. He let out a huge sigh as he approached. It was still raining hard, but he got out and got into Steven's car.

"Hey, babe," said Ricky relieved to see his lover.

"'*Hey, babe?*' Ricky, what the hell is wrong with you? You're plopping down in here acting like we are meeting up for a fucking date or something," stated Steven, hardly in the mood for pleasantries.

"Excuse the hell out of me, Steven," stated Ricky.

"We have to stop Ty before he remembers. Look, if he gets his memory back, it's over for us. Everything we worked for will be gone. And I am not going to jail behind some bullshit!" yelled Steven.

"Why are you mad at me? You're the reason we are here! This is your fault. There was no reason for you to act like that, Steven. Then, you didn't even check to see if he was fucking dead!" stated Ricky.

"Fuck that! It's too late to be playing the damn blame game. Look, he doesn't remember what happened. You are the only one that can get close to him. Here," stated Steven, handing Ricky a bag of white powder.

"What the hell is this?" asked Ricky.

"This is enough medication to kill Ty. I want you to call him and say you lost your phone. Make sure that you act surprised and shit. Tell him you never saw him, and put this in his drink," stated Steven.

"Have you lost your damn mind? What am I supposed to do if he remembers what happened the second he sees me? No, hell no! I'm not going to do it! I don't want him dead, Steven!" yelled Ricky.

"You don't have a fucking choice! We're going to finish what we started," stated Steven.

"We didn't start anything. You did this. You did all of this," stated Ricky, hoping Steven would mistake the tears in his eyes for the rain that soaked him.

"I did all of this with your help. And if Ty remembers, we both are going to jail. Is that what you want? To go to jail for attempted murder and robbery?" asked Steven.

Ricky didn't answer. He just sat there, looking out of the window. The storm represented so much. He knew that his lying ways would catch up to him eventually. He'd already lost Laila. Even though they mostly fought, he could not say it was all of her fault.

"Ricky, you have to do this. There is no other choice. Ty could remember at any minute. How are you going to explain it to him or to the police? I'm telling you. This stuff will finish what we started," Steven stated as he took the bag out of Ricky's hand and held it in the air. After marveling at it, he placed it back in Ricky's hand.

"Okay, suppose I go over there. What the fuck do I tell Toni?" asked Ricky.

"I don't know, and I don't care what you tell her. Just come up with something to get her out of the house," stated Steven.

"I can't do this! I won't, Steven. Maybe he won't remember. Maybe…" reasoned Ricky.

"Maybe his ass will remember, and we will go to jail! We can't afford a maybe. If he's dead, our problems will be over," stated Steven.

"Our problems will not be over. They will never be over, Steve. Did you forget that you're about to be married? What am I supposed to do with my life, huh?" stated Ricky.

Steven didn't answer. He was out of justification where he and Maya were concerned. He loved her, and he loved Ricky.

The men sat in silence until the thunder clapped. Ricky looked at Steven. All of the drama had made him horny. He put the bag on the floor, grabbed the back of Steven's head, and looked into his eyes. Ricky knew Steven knew what he needed in order to convince him to go along with the new plan.

Steven slowly began rubbing Ricky's bulge. Once he felt Ricky rise completely, he pulled out his dick. It was at full salute. He grabbed a towel from his back seat, covered his head and penetrated his mouth with all of Ricky's shaft.

Steven bobbed his head up and down slowly. He was careful not to gag. He could tell by Ricky's moans that his head game was intact. He continued slowly sucking and licking until Ricky exploded in his mouth. He swallowed all of him and sucked him back hard.

After two more rounds of deep-throat action, Ricky stated, "Fine, I'll do it."

Chapter Eight

Maya

Feeling a little tipsy, Maya stumbled off of her sofa and into her bathroom. She knew it was getting close to the time Steven would be picking her up. She undressed and looked at herself in the mirror. She thought of herself as beautiful. She smiled and felt happy.

Her happiness began to fade as thoughts of what she overheard Steven tell Ricky replayed in her mind, though. As much as she tried to force it out, it invaded every fiber of her being. The mere thought of it made her feel sick. She could even smell the mothballs from the closet.

She had so many questions. And she had so many unresolved feelings toward Steven. She knew she would never say anything to him about them.

She looked at herself in the mirror again after the re-alization. The person staring back at her would never be desperate enough to settle for a man who she didn't love. She wanted to return to the past and forget the present.

She brushed her teeth, showered once more, and be-gan getting ready for her night with Steven. She forced the overheard conversation out of her mind and concentrated on her future. As she applied her makeup, she heard a knock on the door.

He's early, she thought. "Just a minute, babe!" she yelled.

She put on her silk black robe and headed for the door. Steven was looking lickable. He had on a light-blue blazer, white V neck T-shirt, and jeans.

"Well, hello, sexy. I hope you don't mind, but I bought dinner," he said, holding out a bag of food.

"No, I don't mind. It's raining anyway. What did you get?" asked Maya as the two embraced.

"I got some of your favorite sushi and a nice bottle of white wine," he stated as he placed the food on the counter.

"Sounds good to me. Just let me get dressed, and I'll…"

Steven interrupted. "What you have on is fine." He walked over to her. Maya's pussy throbbed as he began kissing her.

He pulled the belt on her robe, exposing her naked body, picked her up, and carried her outside to her balcony. The rain came down and cascaded on Maya's body. The moonlight made Maya's nipples glisten as Steven sucked them.

Their passion was undeniable. His slid two fingers inside her to feel her juices. Maya gasped at how wet she'd become. He bent her over the balcony and glided in her with a little bit of force. It felt so good to Maya. She let out a loud moan and didn't give a fuck who heard or who was watching. She just marveled at the fact that she was getting good dick and her best friend was miserable.

She turned around, stopping the deep thrusts, and fell to her knees. His dick was still creamy from her, so she stroked him while the rain washed it off. She then took all of Steven in her mouth and gave one of the best head performances ever. She had to let him know that he could be fine without Ricky. Her head bobbed back and forth on Steven. He tasted divine. She allowed him to navigate her head as she continued licking and gulping his precum and all of his shaft. She liked the fact that Steven kept his privates neatly trimmed. She absolutely hated a man with a bush everywhere.

Once he came all over the floor of the balcony, he sat in the chair and lifted up one of Maya's legs to his shoulder. He began tasting every bit of her. His tongue darted in and out of her, causing her to come for minutes. He slowly pulled her down onto his dick.

Steven wasn't working with a monster, but he definitely had enough to satisfy Maya. She slid down on him and began riding him. He felt so good. They forgot about the rain. Getting wet took on a whole new meaning. They'd both missed each other, and their bodies agreed.

As Steven sucked on her breasts, Maya imagined Ty's face. She began bouncing up and down, faster and faster, until they both came. As the two tried to catch their breath, Maya's mind suddenly drifted back to the first time she saw Ty after their breakup.

A few weeks after the whole movie fiasco, Maya was walking to class. It was cold, and she made a mental note to purchase another scarf. She'd managed to go the entire day without any thoughts of Ty or Toni.

After getting a mocha latte from Martin's Coffee Shop, she saw Ty in the seating area of Gillespie Hall, reading. Her first thought was to go the other way, but she decided to face him. She'd just gotten her hair done and was feeling cute that day anyway. She couldn't have imagined a better time to run into her ex.

"Hi, Ty! How are you?" she asked.

"Oh, hey, Maya. I'm good. Just studying for my English literature exam this Friday. How are you?" he asked. He couldn't help but to admire how good and well put together she looked.

Maya just looked at him. She didn't know how to respond. Every fiber in her being wanted him. "I'm good. I've been studying too. Well, take care," she stated while turning away.

"Hey, hold up a minute, Maya," Ty said as he ran over to her. "I'm sorry, Maya. I'm so sorry. I never meant for any of this shit to happen. You have to believe that," stated Ty, looking concerned.

"I'm sure you didn't, Ty, but it happened. Just answer this one thing for me. How could you do me like this? All I ever wanted to do was love you," stated Maya. Tears formed in her eyes, so she turned her head to avoid him seeing them fall.

If it was one thing Ty hated, it was seeing a woman cry. He reached out and hugged her. "Listen to me, okay? It wasn't me. It was Toni. Toni came on to me. She just caught me slipping. I went over there to wait on you, but she was in her robe. She started kissing me, and she even sucked my dick, Maya. I just got caught up in the moment," Ty stated, making sure he left out the fact that he'd been flirting with Toni months prior.

"You're lying! It takes two, Ty. I didn't catch Toni coming on to you. I caught you fucking my best friend!" she screamed. A few students quickly walked by, trying to avoid overhearing their conversation. Some laughed while others stood there gawking. Ty pulled Maya farther down the hall.

"Maya, please! Look, I'm sorry. I told you that it was all Toni's fault. She'd been coming on to me for months. I tried to tell her to leave me alone, but she seduced me," lied Ty.

"That lying bitch! I knew she fucked you on purpose. Then had the nerve to meet me to apologize," stated Maya, finally believing Ty.

"That's why I can't be with you. That's why I chose her. I know that I'd made the biggest mistake," said Ty, looking defeated and hoping Maya was buying his bullshit. The truth of the matter was too much for him to face.

"Ty, you knew what we had. There was no way I would not have forgiven you, even if it was my best friend. I loved you. I still love you, Ty," stated Maya, reaching out for him to oblige her request. But he didn't. He pulled back his arm from her grasp and stated that although he loved her, he had feelings for Toni now and just couldn't keep going back and forth between the two.

Maya didn't even wait for him to finish. She just walked away. She couldn't hear anymore. Ty didn't stop her that time either. He just stood there, out of lies and excuses.

Maya opened her eyes as she heard Steven call her name. The memory of that day made her despise Toni a bit more. *The fucking nerve of that bitch*, she thought.

After drying off, Maya and Steven made their way to the kitchen to enjoy the sushi he's brought. In between bites of her lion roll and kani salad, Maya listened to Steven's lies about his business trip.

Chapter Nine

Toni

"Well, hello, Mildred. How are you doing?" asked Toni, trying her best to at least be cordial. She didn't have a problem with Mildred, but she knew the disdain her mother-in-law harbored toward her.

"Toni, it's always a pleasure. I'm good, which is more than I can say for my poor son. Where have you been?" asked Mildred.

"Oh, I went to get some coffee," Toni said as she held up her now-cold cup of java.

"They have coffee right over there, Toni. I mean seriously, dear. Your husband was almost killed. You could be at the funeral home planning his funeral right now. You should be by his side. Not in line for Starbucks coffee," stated Mildred.

"Mildred, I have been here. I've been here since early this morning. I called you here, remember?" asked Toni.

"Oh, don't get smart with me, missy. I have a good mind to tell you what I really think about you, but I won't, for Ty's sake. I've been married over twenty-five years, and believe me, Starbucks would be the last thing on my mind if something like this happened to my Jerome," she stated.

"Look, it's been a really long day. I just needed a break. This is a lot for us right now. I am just trying to be there for him the best way I know how. And honestly, Mildred, I shouldn't have to be out here explaining myself to you, if you want to know the truth," stated Toni, tired of Mildred's shit.

"Excuse me," said Mildred with a disgusted look on her face. She went back into Ty's room, leaving Toni in the hall.

Toni couldn't move. She just stood there, tired and confused. Ever since she and Ty had been dating, she'd always tried to bond with Mildred, but to no avail.

Ty always dismissed the disdain between the two. He would make excuses and blame Toni for always reading too much into it. When Toni would ask him to confront his mother, he would always change the subject. This ongoing silent argument, so to speak, had lasted throughout the years.

Toni decided that a fight with Mildred would prove too much today. She opted to call and check on her daughter instead. She pressed the elevator button to go back to the Starbucks area. With her head down, looking for her cell, she didn't even notice Benjamin as she stepped of the elevator.

Benjamin was the brother of Gloria, the woman who did alterations for Toni. He was around five eleven. His skin was light, as if he'd been kissed by a peach. His hair was black, low cut, and wavy. His eyes were light gray. He had an extremely athletic build.

When Toni had needed someone to alter her wedding dress, the lady at the local bridal store suggested Gloria. The lady raved about how Gloria fixed a bride's dress twenty-four hours before her wedding. Toni called Gloria and made an appointment the very next day. She figured anyone who could do that could certainly let out a wedding gown and add some sort of style to it.

The next day, Toni was greeted by a sexy man when she entered the shop. He flashed a gorgeous smile at her and told her that Gloria was finishing up with a client in the back. He introduced himself as Benjamin and explained that he was Gloria's brother. The two chatted a bit before Gloria came out. He told Toni that he'd seen lots of brides in his day but none as beautiful as her.

Toni blushed and thanked Benjamin. When Gloria came out, he excused himself to deliver some finished dresses for Gloria. He kissed Toni's hand and left.

"Well, my brother seems to be quite taken with you!" laughed Gloria as she inspected Toni's dress.

"No, he's just being nice." Toni smiled.

"Honey, I've been his sister a mighty long time. My brother is taken with you. I could see it all in his eyes. He didn't want to leave," stated Gloria as she measured Toni.

"You do not have anything to worry about. In a few days, I'll be a happily married woman," stated Toni.

"I'm happy for you, honey. I wish my brother would find him someone. He's had a hard time in the love department. He has never been married. Bad relationship a few years ago. His then girlfriend pinned a child on him that turned out to be not his. He was devastated. That bitch still has the nerve to come by here for alterations too," stated Gloria with a frown.

"Wow, she definitely has some nerve. That's very unfortunate. He's a handsome man. I hope he can get over it. What happened with the child?" asked Toni as she removed her shoes.

"It was a little boy. He was four when Benjamin found out that he wasn't his. Took the boy to the doctor, somehow found out his blood type, and was shocked that it was different from his. This made him sneak and do a DNA test. It was a damn mess, girl. He still keeps in contact with him, though. He got too attached to just leave him." Gloria looked sad as she revealed truths about her brother.

"Damn, that's pretty noble of him. I know plenty of men who would have just said 'Fuck it,'" said Toni.

"You and me both. Now, sugar, tell me how you'd like me to alter this," stated Gloria.

Benjamin always flirted with Toni. He would make a point to compliment her every chance he would get. He would help deliver clothes and clean up Gloria's shop when she would get backed up. Although Toni found him very attractive, she always reminded him that she was very much a married woman.

"Well, hi, Miss Lady!" he stated with a gorgeous smile.

"Hey, Ben. What are you doing way up here?" asked Toni while giving him a hug. Her nostrils were infused with the smell of Giorgio Armani's Acqua di Gio. She inhaled deeply.

"I'm here visiting my aunt. She had a slight heart attack earlier this week, and this is my first chance to get up here," he stated.

"Oh, I'm sorry to hear that. I saw Gloria yesterday, and she didn't mention it," Toni said.

"Well, it's my aunt on my dad's side. We have different fathers. I don't think Gloria even knows, come to think of it. I haven't been by there this week. I've been working a lot lately," stated Benjamin.

"Where are you working now?" asked Toni.

"I'm back with my old insurance company. Trying to be an agent was too expensive for me, but I'll get there," said Benjamin.

"Well, how is your aunt doing?" asked Toni.

"Oh, she's fine. She's almost sixty-five and is still as feisty as ever!" he laughed.

"That's good to hear," Toni said, still worried.

"So what are you doing all the way up here?" asked Benjamin.

"My husband was the victim of a robbery last night. Someone bashed his head in, and he can't even remember what happened. The police found him in the trunk of his car," she said as her eyes filled with tears. The realness of it all plus the petty drama between her and her mother-in-law overwhelmed Toni. She couldn't hold her emotions in anymore.

Benjamin grabbed her as she cried. Although upset, she couldn't help but notice how safe and secure she felt in his arms. She couldn't remember the last time Ty made her feel safe like that.

"Listen to me. It's going to be all right," he stated.

"I hope so, Ben. I really do. I just feel so alone and helpless right now," she stated in between sobs.

"Let's go over here and sit down," he stated after handing her some tissues he saw on a table.

They walked over to the lounge area. There, Toni began to tell Benjamin about her past twenty-four hours, the whole Maya drama, and her mother-in-law. Benjamin just sat there listening, nodding his head, and imagining her pussy on top of his dick.

Chapter Ten

Ty

Bad boys, bad boys, whatcha gonna do,
whatcha gonna do when they come for you.

—*Inner Circle, "Bad Boys"*

After leaving the hospital, the detectives decided to get some food and go over the notes from the case. The Dunkin' Donuts wasn't too far from the hospital. They thought it would be a good spot just in case Ty got his memory back.

The detectives went over their notes and started trying to come up with different theories as to what may have happened to Ty. They went over different crimes that had taken place in that area and nearby cities. Nothing was similar to Ty's situation, though. Most robbers in the area left their victims unharmed or mildly injured at best. It just didn't make sense that they would go to such extremes to cover up a simple robbery.

They started looking into Ty's finances. He wasn't that well off, so being the target of money couldn't be the reason. Plus, he wasn't even from that area. His car was an average car too.

It just didn't make sense. Then, their theories went to his wife, Ricky, and Maya. They tried to piece together what little they knew about each of them. Still, no clear motive stuck out.

The location was the main thing that pulled them more toward Ricky's direction. He lived in the area, Ty and Ricky were best friends, and he acted strange as hell when they told him about Ty. He hadn't come to visit either. The detectives were interrupted by Detective Reed's phone ringing.

"This is Detective Reed. Really? We'll be right there," he stated.

"What? Did you get a new lead in the Weeks case?" asked Detective Price in between doughnut bites.

"Yes, apparently Mr. Weeks got a ticket warning yesterday not too far from here. The officer who wrote it up is down at the station right now," stated Detective Reed.

Once the detectives arrived at the station, Officer Bakersfield was waiting. He told the detectives that Ty was speeding and seemed very distracted. They asked if Ty was alone, and the officer said yes. He said that he noticed Ty turn around in the opposite direction of where he was going originally. The detectives then determined that the direction was heading back toward Ricky's house. The detectives decided to pay Ricky another visit.

When they got there, they knocked for a few minutes until they were sure he wasn't home. They decided to look around. They checked the exterior of the house, looking for blood, broken glass, or anything that would result from a struggle. Nothing seemed out of the ordinary except the faint smell of bleach.

The detectives walked toward the back of the house. Detective Price noticed the trash can. He lifted the lid and saw something wrapped up. He put on some plastic gloves and inspected the object.

"Reed, looks like a broken lamp," Detective Price stated as he continued his inspection.

"Oh, yeah. Well, wrap it back up so we can secure a search warrant from the judge. You know how the lieutenant is with all of the legal compliance bullshit," stated Detective Reed.

"So just leave it here? Leave potential evidence?" asked Detective Price.

"We don't have a choice. I don't want to hear that crap about how we didn't follow proper procedure and protocol. They just don't let us be detectives anymore. I told my old lady that I may need to find another department," stated Detective Reed.

"I know, man. It's fucking ridiculous! How in the hell do they expect us to solve this shit if we can't even secure evidence?" asked Detective Price.

"Exactly! Let's call it in and go pay Maya Fisher a visit tomorrow morning. By the time it's ready, we can swing back by to get it and can do an official search," stated Detective Reed.

Detective Price reluctantly wrapped up the lamp and closed the lid. He knew they were making a terrible mistake. He just hoped the search warrant was approved soon.

Chapter Eleven

Ricky

I can't believe what I just agreed to do, Ricky thought as he drove in and out of traffic. He rolled down all of his windows when the rain stopped and allowed the moist air to infuse his nostrils. He inhaled deeply, trying to calm his pounding heart.

The small bag of white powder sat in the cup holder. He wanted to throw it out. He picked it up and just stared at it.

How am I going to do this? he thought.

His stomach growled. He hadn't eaten anything since he'd left the Hamilton that morning. He decided on a veggie burger combo from Burger King.

After eating, he began going over what he'd say to Toni. He knew that he needed to act surprised and upset. He wasn't sure if the detectives even told Toni and Ty that they paid him a visit or not. He just wanted to make sure that he reiterated that he never saw Ty.

He made several attempts of calling Toni. He'd dial and then hang up or dial and just stare before pressing the send button. Finally, he allowed the phone to ring. Just when he was about to hang up, Toni answered.

"Hello, Ricky, are you okay?" Toni asked.

"Hey, Toni, I'm so sorry. I left my phone at the gym yesterday and just got your missed calls and messages. What is going on? Where is Ty?" he asked as if he were working on his first Oscar.

Toni completely broke down on the phone. "Ricky, Ty is in the hospital. He was robbed and left for dead last night. Oh, God! They found him in the trunk of his car," Toni managed to say in between sobs.

"What the fuck? I'm sorry for my language. Who did it? Is he okay?" Rick asked.

"We don't know who did it. The police are investigating but..." Toni couldn't continue. It seemed like just speaking about the event was proving to be too much for her to Ricky.

"But what, Toni? But what?" asked Ricky.

"Ty can't remember what happened! He has short-term memory loss," Toni explained.

"Jesus Christ, Toni! I'm so sorry. Where are you? I'm on my way over there," he stated, silently praying for her to not take him up on his offer.

"We're at the hospital not far from you, but visiting hours are over. The doctor said that there is nothing else they can do. We're hoping that he can go home tomorrow," Toni stated.

"Damn, I'm so sorry, Toni. I should have been there for you. I should have been there for Ty. I know you must be exhausted. Let me make it up to you," he stated.

"No, it's all right. Ty's been asking about you, though, and so have the detectives. Ty said that he was meeting up with you yesterday. You didn't see him at all?" asked Toni.

Ricky remained silent. He knew what he said was absolutely critical, and he didn't want to mess up or forget one single word.

"Um, no, Toni. I...I didn't see him. I haven't even talked to Ty. We were all supposed to meet up at the tux fitting today, but Steven texted me that it was canceled. Is Maya there with you?" Ricky asked, hoping to change the subject.

"No, I haven't even spoken to her today. I've called and left messages. She finally called me back, but I'm not up for her personality right now," stated Toni bluntly.

"Hell, I'm never up for her personality, and neither was Laila," he joked, relieved he'd shifted the conversation off of him.

"Oh, speaking of Laila, I ran into her at the hospital earlier today," stated Toni.

"You. Ran. Into. Laila?" Ricky asked with his eyes widened.

"Yeah, her sister had a baby today. She's up here or was up here. I saw her at the Starbucks downstairs. She... well, never mind." Toni stopped herself. She wasn't even sure why she even blurted out the fact that she had seen Laila, given the divorce and all.

"She what?" asked Ricky.

"She said something about Steven, but I guess it really doesn't matter now," said Toni.

"What did she say?" asked Ricky as he pulled into his driveway. His heart was beating fast. He hoped that she didn't tell her about the real reason they divorced.

"She said that Steven was the reason why y'all got divorced or something to that effect. She told me to tell Maya to be careful, which was strange considering their history," said Toni.

"Be careful about what? Steven? Why in the hell would she even say that? That woman will blame everyone but herself," stated Ricky, successfully hiding the fact that he was now fuming.

"Yeah, I just figured he gave you some legal advice or something. You know, with him being a lawyer and all. She didn't go into details or anything like that. Anyway, I'm about to try to get some rest. I'll tell Ty I spoke to you and that you're all right," Toni said.

"Okay, then! Hey, I'm going to send you to the spa tomorrow," said Ricky.

"The spa? How am I going to do all of that when I'll be taking care of Ty?" she asked.

"If he gets out tomorrow, I'll come over and hang out with him until you get back. It's the least I can do, and I'm not taking no for an answer. Just call me, okay?" he asked.

"Okay, and Ricky, thanks for being a great friend to us. Bye now," Toni stated and hung up.

Thanks for being a great friend to us, he thought as he glared at his phone. He gathered his things along with his

Burger King bag and headed for his trash can behind the house, hanging his head in shame. He didn't want to do anything but sleep. His mind, body, and soul were completely exhausted.

Chapter Twelve

Maya

Looking out on the morning rain, I used to feel so uninspired.

—*Aretha Franklin, "Natural Woman"*

As the rain drizzled on the city of Birmingham, Maya opened her eyes to a dreary Saturday morning. Steven turned his back as the sun barely shone through the curtains. She decided not to wake him. Instead she brushed her teeth, showered, and put on a pot of coffee.

She checked her phone for messages. She had a voice mail from the wedding chapel. She decided to listen to it later as she scrolled to see if Toni had texted or called her back.

Hmm, no call back. I hope Ty is okay, she thought, realizing for the first time that she was somewhat concerned.

She quickly dismissed her feelings and searched through her fridge to find something to cook for breakfast. She decided on omelets, grits, and fruit. Steven always liked her cooking, so she wanted to remind him of how every Saturday morning would be once they were married.

Speaking of married, she grabbed her cell and listened to the voice mail from the chapel. It was the pastor's wife, adamantly apologizing about mixing up the dates. Apparently, June 7 was no longer available. She also said that June 17 was available.

Maya slammed down her phone and let out a huge sigh. She hated that she'd fired her coordinator. Now she would have to basically change her honeymoon and move-in dates. She was also worried about Steven's reaction, the whole Ty drama, and how she needed to make it down the aisle.

After putting the final touches on the breakfast tray, Maya walked in the room. Steven was still asleep.

"Wake up, sleepyhead. Steven, I made us some breakfast," she said, opening the curtains. The dust flew. She made a mental note to wash them later.

"Um, good morning, baby. That smells nice. What do we have here, huh?" he said, wiping his eyes.

"Well, we have omelets with spinach, mozzarella cheese, mushrooms, and onions. I also made buttered grits and coffee and cut up some fruit," she said, admiring her accomplishment.

"Thanks, it looks delicious," he said, taking in a mouthful of grits.

The two began eating and discussing plans for the day. Maya was a bit upset about Steven's reaction to the whole change-the-date thing. He acted like he didn't care one way or the other.

He noticed her mood change. "Wow, breakfast was delicious. What's the matter, Maya?" he asked while gently rubbing her cheek.

This man was sexy.

"Your nonchalant attitude toward the date change is what the matter is," she snapped.

"Babe, you know I want nothing more than to make you Mrs. Sims. It'll happen. Trust me," he said as he began kissing her on her shoulder.

The words *trust me* stabbed Maya in her already broken heart. *How in the fuck can I trust you when you've been lying to me? I don't know if you're gay. If you're fucking Ricky. I don't even know why the hell you tried to kill Ty*, she thought as his tongue trailed from her shoulder to her inner thighs.

She could feel herself becoming wet. Steven slowly pulled her panties to the side and began licking her clit. He moaned as he savored her juices. He grabbed a strawberry from the bowl of fruit and dipped it in her pussy. Maya was turned on even more when he ate it.

He pulled her panties down and immediately slid his dick inside her. The passion was so intense that making love was simply out of the question. He pulled her legs over his shoulders and began going deeper and deeper. Maya moaned loudly with each thrust. He picked her up and began bouncing her up and down on his dick.

All thoughts of his dishonesty disappeared. She closed her eyes and imagined that the man fucking her was everything she'd ever dreamed. She imagined that she was really in love and really excited about the man she was going to marry. The thoughts of true love allowed her to take the pounding Steven was supplying.

They both came while standing up. He gently laid her down and left to take a shower. He left with no words, no kisses, and no cuddling. She was glad that he didn't. She simply didn't want to continue with *appearances too*.

Maya was startled as she heard a knock at the door. *Who in the hell could that be at this time of morning*? she thought. She grabbed her robe and headed for the door.

Steven checked his phone while in the bathroom. He noticed that he had two missed calls from Ricky. *If this motherfucker messes this up, I'm going to have to kill his ass too*, he thought as he pressed send.

"What's up, Ricky?" asked Steven.

"What's up is that bitch ex-wife of mine. How about she told Toni that you were the reason why we divorced!" yelled Ricky.

"She told Toni about us? You talked to Toni? Ty remember anything?" Steven whispered, desperate for answers to each question.

"No, he doesn't remember. Hell, Toni didn't say that she mentioned us, but that shit might make her suspicious. She told her to tell Maya to be careful about you. I don't even know why she would say anything to Toni anyway. And why the fuck are you whispering?" Ricky said, clearly pissed off.

"That sorry bitch. Don't worry about it. I'll take care of her ass," Steven stated calmly, making sure he ignored Ricky's question. The last thing he needed was to piss him off more by telling him that he was at Maya's. He needed Ricky to pull off Ty's murder today.

"Whatever. I'm waiting for Toni to call me so that I can go visit Ty. I'm scared. I don't know if I can go through with this," stated Ricky.

"Don't bitch up, Ricky. Our future depends on it," stated Steven as he hung up the phone, his thoughts shifting toward Laila.

Chapter Thirteen

Toni

Toni sat quietly at the hospital pharmacy. Ty's doctor was allowing him to go home this morning, so she wanted to go ahead and get his prescription filled.

The waiting area was full of all types of people. Toni looked at them and tried to guess their ailments. She saw an older guy standing near the counter and guessed he was getting some Viagra. She noticed a younger girl who looked no older than twenty-five. *She's probably here for birth control or Plan B. Oh, to be young again*, thought Toni as she laughed to herself.

"Ty Weeks, your prescription is now ready. Please make your way to window five," said the lady on the loudspeaker.

Toni walked to window five and explained that she was picking up the prescription for her husband. The pharmacist told her that the doctor had prescribed a medicine called Demerol. She explained to Toni that the medicine would help with Ty's pain. She also warned that it could get addictive if not used correctly.

Toni thanked the pharmacist and headed toward the elevator. She noticed her cell blinking and saw that she still had a voice mail. She exhaled as she pressed play. She rolled her eyes at Maya's pathetic excuse, dropped her phone back in her purse, and pressed the button to Ty's floor.

Ty's parents had left late last night to go get Jessica from Mrs. Carol. They all agreed that Jessica should go back with them for a few days. Toni and Ty needed to adjust. Toni didn't want her baby to leave, but due to the circumstances she thought it was best. Plus, she knew Mrs. Carol needed a break.

She loved her daughter but knew she could be a handful at times. She thought about how Maya wouldn't watch Jessica for her one day.

Spring was in the air, and Toni was in desperate need of a break. It had been months since she'd gotten her hair, nails, and toes done. It was even longer than that when it came to a professional massage.

She called around to see if any spas had openings. She wanted to do an entire spa day package that would include lunch. She finally found an opening with Santa Fe Day Spa on Highway 280.

After a sigh of relief, she called Ty to see if he had to work that Saturday. He told her that he did and couldn't take off. Toni felt defeated. She never did anything for herself, and the one time she wanted to, she couldn't.

She thought about Mrs. Carol but remembered that she was gone to visit her sister in California. The only other alternative was Maya.

Maya had never actually volunteered to keep Jessica. In fact, the only time she kept her was for a few hours when Toni had strep throat. Maya called over and over until Ty came to pick up Jessica.

After a deep sigh, Toni dialed Maya's number and hoped that her best friend would act as such on that day.

"Hey, Toni. What's up?" Maya asked, sounding as if she were still asleep.

"Hey, Maya. Nothing much, just folding up some towels and watching a little TV. What do you have going on this Saturday?" asked Toni.

"Nothing that I know of. I was supposed to show the McKinley house, but my client canceled. I hate it too because it is to die for. Not to mention the commission would give me the opportunity to purchase that new Mercedes-Benz I've been admiring. I'll probably just go shopping or something. It's supposed to be a nice sale at Victoria's Secret. If not, I'll probably just chill. Steven gets back that night," said Maya.

"The McKinley house? Isn't that the one we did the open house for?" asked Toni.

"Yes, sure is. It's a beauty," stated Maya.

"I remember that day. I was up all night baking cookies and cupcakes for that open house. It better sell," joked Toni.

"Those were some good cookies and cupcakes too!" snickered Maya.

"Yes, indeed. I'd love to have a house like that. I'd walk around all day in my feather-adorned pink robe!" laughed Toni.

"I heard that," stated Maya as she let out a slight chuckle. It was obvious that she was faking it. She didn't see the humor in Toni not working and being able to lounge around all day.

"Would you mind watching Jessica for me on Saturday, since you don't have plans?" asked Toni. "Ty gets off at three, and he can stop by and get her afterward."

"Watch Jessica? For what? And what do you have to do anyway?" asked Maya with an obvious attitude.

"Maya, I just need a break. I need a spa day. You know, with being a full-time mommy, I never get a chance to relax. I just…"

"Um, no, I actually don't know. And I'm not going to be able to watch her," interrupted Maya.

"Girl, you just said that you didn't have anything planned. Victoria's Secret is open until like nine at night. Would it kill you to spend some time with your goddaughter?" asked Toni.

"Oh, don't try to lay that goddaughter crap on me. You don't want me to spend time with her. You just need a babysitter. Sorry, but us working people rest on the weekends. Talk to you later, girl," stated Maya as she hung up the phone.

Toni just looked at her cell as the call ended. Maya had hurt her feelings. She started to call her back and curse her out but decided against it. As much as she hated to admit it, Maya was right. Jessica was her child and her responsibility. Being friends with Maya didn't obligate her to keep Toni's child.

A few moments later, Laila called Toni and asked if she could borrow her Prada bag for an event in Birmingham on Friday night. Toni said sure and asked about the event. Laila told her that it was a natural hair mixer. When Toni mentioned how exciting it sounded, Laila invited her to come also. Toni said, on one condition.

Laila ended up spending the night that Friday and stayed with Jessica until Ty got back home from work that Saturday. Toni ended up having her spa day after all.

Toni smiled as she stepped off the elevator. *See how God works*, she thought.

Chapter Fourteen

Ty

Ty pulled the thin hospital sheets up closer to his chest. He hated how cold they kept hospitals. Every time he inhaled the cold air, he could feel the pain in his head. He wondered what the fuck he had been hit with.

That shit must have been a damn steel pipe or something. What else could knock somebody's whole memory away? he thought.

The bandages were tight on his head as well. He was sure all of the added pressure was contributing to the pain. He beeped for his nurse.

"Yes, Mr. Weeks?" asked the nurse over the room speaker.

"Hey, will someone bring me a hand mirror please?" he asked.

"Certainly, sir," the nurse stated.

A few moments later, a lady came in with a small hand mirror. Ty held it up to his face and couldn't believe his reflection. His face looked distorted. His eyes were black, and the bandages literally covered his entire head. The more he looked at himself, the more enraged he became.

He wished he had the slightest idea of who'd done this to him. He was ready to find someone. He wanted justice. He heard his hospital door open. It was the doctor.

"Hi, Mr. Weeks. I'm Dr. Davie. How's that head feeling?" he asked.

"Hi, it's bothering me. The pain is pretty bad," explained Ty.

"Well, I wrote you a prescription that should help with the pain. Just remember to be cautious when using it," instructed the doctor.

"So just lay it on me, straight man. Am I going to ever fucking remember what happened to me?" asked Ty.

"Unfortunately, I don't have the answer, Mr. Weeks. Most people will regain partial memory while some never remember. These things just take time. You have to take it easy and allow your brain to heal," replied the doctor, not looking older than thirty.

"Take it easy? How can I take it easy when I was found in a fucking trunk with a gash in my head and don't even know who put me there?" Ty yelled.

The doctor apologized again, gave Ty some final instructions, and left the room. He wasn't in the mood to argue with patients that day. He just wanted to take a smoke break.

Toni walked in after the doctor left. She'd overheard their conversation in the hallway. She looked totally embarrassed.

"Ty, what is the matter with you? You can't go off on people who are trying to help you, let alone the doctor," Toni stated while shaking her head.

"Don't tell me what I can't do, okay? You're not the one who has a damn gash in your head or memory loss. Just shut the hell up!" he yelled. Ty didn't mean to take it out on his wife, but he was so frustrated. The thought of almost dying and then not being able to remember was taking its toll on him. He loved her, but he wanted her to be upset with him. He didn't want to reason about anything.

"Look, Ty, I know you're upset, but you're taking it out on the wrong people. I didn't put your ass in that trunk, and neither did that poor doctor. I mean, cursing out that doctor was totally unnecessary. I should go find him and apologize," stated Toni.

"Apologize for what?" asked Ty.

"What do you mean, for what? Apologize for the way you spoke to him. It was not called for at all, Ty," stated Toni.

"What was not called for was somebody trying to kill me. I don't fucking bother nobody. I go to work, and I go home. I don't deserve to be here losing time off from work," stated Ty.

"Just be glad that you are alive, Ty. Just be glad that you are not in a coma or something. I understand your frustrations, baby, but you have to take the good with the bad," Toni said.

"You just don't get it! I don't remember what happened! You can't understand how that feels. Why aren't you angry?" asked Ty.

"I am angry, but I'm also relived. Ty, you could have been killed. I guess that outweighs it for me," stated Toni.

Just then, the nurse came in with Ty's release papers along with an orderly who had a wheelchair. She went over some additional instructions while Toni gathered the rest of their things. The orderly assisted Ty into the wheelchair.

Toni went ahead of them to go get their car. She was confused and exhausted. Sleeping on a small hospital cot is far from a stay at the Marriott.

She checked her phone and noticed she had a text message from Benjamin. He'd insisted she give him her number after their conversation yesterday. He asked if she was feeling better. She let out a deep sigh and simply replied no.

As she hurried to the hospital entrance, she had to stop herself from crying. Everything was just falling apart. Her happy life wasn't very happy at all, and she was damn tired of keeping up *appearances too*.

Ty looked upset as the orderly helped him get into the car. He thanked him as Toni prepared to drive off. "Toni, have you heard from Ricky?" asked Ty.

"Yeah, he called last night. I was going to tell you, but you were asleep when I came back. And it slipped my mind this morning," she said.

"Well, what did he say? Did I go see him, talk to him, or what?" he asked.

"He said he never saw or talked to you, Ty. He said that he left his phone at the gym. That's why he never answered. I texted him a few minutes ago and told him you were discharged. He's on his way to the house," she said.

"Good, maybe he will be able to shed some light on something. Lord knows you weren't any help," Ty stated.

"Ty, I wasn't with you. I can only tell you what I know," Toni stated, unsure if she should reciprocate his attitude.

"Just drive, Toni. I'm about to go to sleep. My head is killing me again. Where's my prescription? The doctor said it was for pain," he said as he looked around the car.

Toni simply pointed to the bag on the floor and kept driving. She didn't even notice her cell blinking with another text from Benjamin.

Chapter Fifteen

Ricky

Ricky was glad it was trash day. He desperately wanted to get rid of the lamp Steven had used to hit Ty. He quickly pulled the large trash can to the curb and checked his mailbox.

More mail for Laila. Why won't that bitch change her address and her name? She knows she no longer lives here, he thought.

He had a mind to call her and go off about that and her conversation with Toni. He quickly got that idea out of his head, though. The last thing he needed today was to be reminded of his truth. He thought back to the first time he saw her after she'd left.

The house was a mess. He hadn't showered for days. He didn't answer calls or texts from anyone. He wouldn't even talk to Steven. He couldn't tell him what had happened. He was completely lost in his fears of Laila telling everyone what she knew.

The photos remained on the table. Inside of the house were remnants of his life with Laila. She declined to take their marriage and engagement photos off the wall. She wanted him to see the love they once shared that he'd now lost.

He couldn't eat. Couldn't sleep or anything. He worried that his parents would show up unannounced. The disappointment on his dad's face would be too much to bear. He needed to talk to Laila. She wouldn't answer any of her calls. He finally called her sister, Joan.

Joan always cared a lot for Ricky. He helped her with her boys since her husband worked late nights. He would pick them up from school, take them to sports events, and buy them anything they wanted. He was a good uncle.

"Hello, who is this? Sit yo bad ass down, Jeremiah! Your dad is going to tear you up when he gets home! Take that stool off the table. Lord, have mercy. Who is this?" asked Joan again.

"Hey, Joan, it's me," stated Ricky, sounding as if he'd swallowed a mouth full of sawdust.

"Ricky? What's wrong with you? Where are you?" asked Joan, still yelling at her boys in the background.

"I'm at home. Is Laila over there?" asked Ricky.

"Yes, she's here, but why are you calling my phone?" asked Joan.

"She won't answer my calls. Will you please have her call me or at least stop by?" Ricky asked.

"Now, Ricky, you know I try to stay out of grown folks' business. Laila won't even tell us what's going on with y'all. She just showed up with a truck full of her whole house. Now who the hell packs the whole house and asks to stay with somebody? Hell, I have furniture too. I guess my bed wasn't good enough. I tell you the truth," chuckled Joan.

Ricky couldn't help but laugh. Joan had the best sense of humor. She was a comedian and didn't even know it.

"Yeah, I'm sorry about that. She won't talk to me. I haven't seen or heard from her in days. How is she doing?" asked Ricky.

"She's doing all right, I guess. She hasn't really said anything to us. She just stays in the room mostly. Whatever it is, I told her it ain't worth giving up on her husband," stated Joan.

Ricky wished that he could have agreed with her. He honestly knew that this was worth giving up someone. He was more afraid of what Laila would say or who she'd say it to for that matter.

"Joan, please tell Laila to call me. I really need to talk to her. I really need to know that she's all right," stated Ricky.

"Oh all right! I'll tell her. Jeremiah, get that damn dog out of that trash can! Go get my belt. Ricky, I got to go whoop some ass, but I'll tell her what you said. Bye!" stated Joan.

Ricky hung up and shook his head. Joan was hilarious. He sure was going to miss the days of being around her and his nephews.

Later that evening, he heard a car pull up in the driveway. It was Laila. He ran to wash his face and brush his teeth. He hadn't expected her to show up but was glad she had. He needed to do whatever he had to do to convince her to not tell anyone about Steven.

She rang the doorbell. As anxious as he was, he hesitated. He didn't know what to expect. He didn't know what he was going to say to her. He didn't know if he even had the courage to face her. After taking several deep breaths, he finally opened the door.

"Hey, come in," he stated, barely making eye contact.

Laila didn't speak. She just walked in and stood near the entrance with her arms folded. Ricky had forgotten how beautiful she was. Even in her dismay, she was beautiful. He was so wrapped up in Steven, he forgot to even notice her beauty anymore.

"Listen, you have five minutes. What the fuck do you possibly have to say to me?" asked Laila, visibly distraught.

"I'm sorry. Laila, I truly am sorry. I never wanted to hurt you. I want you to know that you did absolutely nothing wrong and that you didn't deserve this," stated Ricky, searching for some sort of sign that she cared.

Laila just stood there, unable to respond. Tears welled up in her eyes, and her lips began to quiver. She actually began shaking.

"Did you use protection, Ricky?" Laila asked.

"Did I what?" asked Ricky.

"Did you use a rubber while you fucked another man, Ricky? Did you?" asked Laila, her eyes searching for the truth.

"Yes, I did. You know I did," Ricky lied. He didn't have the heart to admit anything else to her. He knew she'd been hurt enough.

"I don't know that! I'm going to the doctor tomorrow. If I have anything, you're going to regret it for the rest of your life!" screamed Laila as she turned to leave.

"Laila, wait!" Ricky hollered, grabbing her arm.

"Let go of me! Let go of me, Ricky!" yelled Laila.

He could feel her body trembling. "Laila, you got to believe me. I'm sorry. Please don't ruin me. Don't tell anyone, Laila. I beg you!" cried Ricky.

"So that's it, huh? That's why you needed to talk to me. You don't want to try to save our marriage. You want to save how the world sees you. Just admit it! You are a gay man too scared to show the world who you really are, Ricky. Why marry me, then? Why get my hopes all up that we would have a family together? Why ruin my fucking life because you aren't man enough to live yours?" screamed Laila.

"I love you, Laila. This just happened. And I'm not gay," stated Ricky.

"I'd like to know what the hell you are if you're not gay. And you don't love me. You don't love me. You don't love me, Ricky. I wasn't sure until this very moment, but you never loved me. Let go of my fucking arm!" she yelled. She snatched away from Ricky, ran out of the house, and sped off into the night. Ricky rushed to call Steven. He needed his lover, but he also needed legal advice. He had to find a way to stop Laila. It was then that Steven drew up the gag order for Laila.

Ricky got into his car as the memory from that night began to go away. The car was warm, so he decided to let the windows down. The air was still cool from the rain last night. He inhaled and glanced toward the white bag on his console.

I have to go through with it. There's absolutely no way I can risk Ty remembering, he thought.

He grabbed his cell and made Toni an appointment at her favorite spa. He figured that three hours would be enough time to give Ty the drugs, get rid of the evidence, and leave. He'd simply say that Ty went to sleep and he just left.

Steven hadn't told him what the white powder actually was, anyway. He wasn't even sure what type of reaction the drug would cause. He just trusted his lover.

He hated what he was about to do. One part of him wanted to just go to the police and tell the truth, but he'd already lied to them. It was simply too late. He was in too deep.

His heart pounded as he drove. At times, he was unable to keep a firm grip on the steering wheel. He couldn't drive fast enough.

He went over and over what he was going to say. He even practiced his facial expressions in the visor. He could barely look at himself, though. The reflection reminded him of what he was about to do. He closed his visor and pulled out a blunt he'd rolled earlier.

The aroma was a bit strong, but he didn't care. There was no way he would be able to pull this off without some form of brain manipulation.

After several attempts to find some decent mood music, he opted for his cell. He plugged in his aux cord and finally settled on Devin the Dude's *To Tha X-treme* album. As he inhaled, he imagined the events leading up to his present.

If there was ever a time for a rewind button, now was it. He saw the blood. He saw the pain on his friend's face. Then he saw himself clean up the room.

As "Cooter Brown" played in the background, he reveled at the irony of the lyrics. "Oh life, used to be so wonderful. But ooooh, look at me now."

Yeah, look at me now, he thought as he exhaled the smoke.

Chapter Sixteen

Maya

"Who is it?" Maya asked as she tied her robe.

"Detective Price and Detective Reed here for a Maya Fisher. We're with the Douglasville Police Department," Detective Price stated.

Maya froze dead in her tracks. She repeated the names over and over in her head. She was sure the detectives were here to ask about Steven. Her heart started beating rapidly. She checked to make sure Steven was still in the shower and closed her bedroom door. After a few deep breaths, she opened the door.

"May I help you, detectives?" she asked.

"Miss Fisher, I'm Detective Price, and this is Detective Reed. We'd like to ask you a few questions," stated Detective Price.

"Sure, what can I help you with, Detective Price?" asked Maya reaching out to shake their hands. She didn't dare invite them in because she did not want to alert Steven.

"Miss Fisher, when was the last time you spoke to Toni and Ty Weeks?" asked Detective Reed.

"I spoke with Toni on Thursday evening. She and I took an impromptu trip," laughed Maya.

The detectives didn't find any humor in her statement. In fact, they both gave each other a "she may know more than she's letting on" look. The mood remained awkward.

"Are you aware that your best friend's husband is in the hospital?" asked Detective Reed.

"Why, yes, I am. I tried calling Toni, but she hasn't called me back. I'm planning on going to see them," lied Maya.

"How did you find out what happened?" asked Detective Price.

"I received a voice mail from Toni. I still haven't heard anything, though. Is Ty all right?" she asked.

"I'm afraid not. Someone tried to kill him. He's stable but has short-term memory loss," stated Detective Reed.

"Oh my God! What does short-term memory loss mean?" asked Maya, already knowing the answer.

"It means he can't remember what happened to him, basically," stated Detective Price, visibly irritated.

"I can't imagine. This is so terrible," stated Maya, trying to seem concerned but feeling relieved all at the same time.

"How would you describe your friendship with the Weeks?" asked Detective Price.

"Well, she's my best friend, and I'm hers. I'm her daughter's godmother. We all go way back," she stated.

"So we've heard. How do you feel about her stealing Ty away from you?" asked Detective Price.

"Excuse me? That's all water under the bridge. I'm engaged to be married," gloated Maya, flashing her rock and careful not to mention Steven.

"We'll be in touch and go check on your friend," said Detective Reed as he tipped his hat.

Maya closed the door without saying good-bye. She didn't move. She couldn't. All she could think about was the conversation she'd overheard while she was in Steven's closet.

Her body felt limp. She walked outside on her balcony and looked over the gorgeous skyline of Birmingham. Her mind drifted back to her father, her first day meeting Ty, and the images of Ty fucking Toni.

"Why do I continue to do this to myself? Why am I so unhappy?" she whispered as her tears recreated the look of her robe.

"I have everything I've ever wanted, and now I will lose everything. If Ty remembers, not only will Steven and Ricky go to jail, but I will be the laughingstock of my firm. Toni will have won again. My wedding, my house, my whole life will be destroyed. And I'll end up right back to where I don't want to be. Alone," she whispered. "I have to do something…"

"Maya, who are you talking to? Who was at the door?" asked Steven, interrupting her.

Maya was unsure of what to say next. She knew that telling Steven what she knew about him and Ricky would destroy their relationship. She didn't want him to know that she was so desperate that she would settle for lies and unfaithfulness.

"It was no one," she said, not turning to face him. If he saw her face at that moment, he would know she was being untruthful.

"But I thought I heard you talking to someone," stated Steven.

"It was the wrong apartment. Go back inside, please. I just need a few moments to myself," she said with her back still turned.

"Whatever you say, babe," said Steven, closing the door.

He knew exactly who was there. It never even occurred to him that they would suspect Maya. He loved her, but at least he had another angle to consider if Ricky didn't come through.

Oh well, option B, he thought as he poured himself a glass of water.

Chapter Seventeen

Toni

Toni continued to drive as her mind had thoughts of Ty. She loved him, but she honestly couldn't answer if she was in love anymore. Sure, they enjoyed each other's company, but she purposefully concealed her opinions.

She simply had lost herself. That coupled with the circumstances made her feel invisible at times. She wondered if Ty ever truly saw her as something besides a wife and mother.

He never asked her what she was interested in doing other than being a homemaker. She guessed he just assumed that was all she wanted. She wasn't a part of anything outside of her home. Her experiences only revolved around her family. That's not a terrible thing, but every person needs to explore their interests.

Here she was, a college graduate with nothing to show for her efforts. She often found herself looking through home magazines and would imagine herself listed in the credits. She enjoyed interior design and enjoyed party planning as well.

Every time she would mention her dreams to Ty, he would dismiss the idea and tell her to think about how much time it would take away from their family.

She noticed her cell blinking. Benjamin asked her if there was anything he could do. She replied, *I'll be fine.*

"Ty, we're here," she said as she pressed the send button on her cell.

Ty was still quite groggy from the medicine given to him coupled with his prescription. Toni helped him get settled in his recliner and gathered the rest of their things out of the car. By the time she'd made it back, he was asleep. She decided to take this time to call and check on Jessica and shower.

The hot water felt good. The hospital shower had been terrible: small and very uncomfortable. She figured that she would draw a bath for Ty and bathe him later. After drying off and putting on a very clingy sundress, she heard Ty calling her name.

"Toni, where are you?" he yelled.

"I'm right here. I just took a shower. Ricky is sending me to the spa today," she stated.

"Sending you to the spa for what? Never mind, sit down a minute," stated Ty.

Toni was certainly confused by Ty's behavior. His mood swings were increasing. She exhaled as she sat on the couch facing him, still trying to be the supportive wife.

"Now, you said that I went to work Thursday but I got off early?" he asked.

"Well, I don't know if you got off early or not. You said you were, though," Toni recalled.

"So you and I didn't talk after I got off?" asked Ty.

"No, I called you, but you didn't answer," stated Toni.

"And you said something about you were with Maya?" he asked.

"Yeah, after I got Jessica from school, I had a voice mail from Maya. Rather than listen, I called her back. She couldn't get in touch with Steven and thought he was with Ricky. You know, come to think of it, she said that she overhead Steven yelling at Ricky or some shit. Anyway, I asked Mrs. Carol to keep Jessica for a few hours while we went off to play *Thelma and Louise*." Toni laughed.

"Voice mail? Do you still have it?" asked Ty.

"Yeah, let's see," said Toni. She went and grabbed her cell from her purse. Noticing her texts to Benjamin, she deleted them and pressed her voice mail button.

After hearing Maya's voice, Ty leaned forward. "I'm confused with all of this. The same day she calls you is the same day I get fucked up! It's just not making sense. What happened then?" asked Ty.

"It was nothing, really. We were gone about two hours or so. We kept calling and texting all of you guys. Finally, Steven called Maya back, and we turned around," said Toni.

"Where were you all going? Steven's house?" asked Ty.

"No, we were going to Ricky's house because she called Ricky's phone," Toni recalled.

"Let me get this straight now. Maya called Ricky's phone and thought she heard Steven yell at him?" asked Ty.

"Right, she thought Steven was at Ricky's house cheating on her, and I guess she figured Steven was mad Ricky answered her call. I don't know. It all was crazy as hell. You know how she overreacts and shit. I told her that she needs to trust him," stated Toni nonchalantly.

Before they could continue their conversation, they heard a car pull up. Toni looked out of the window.

"Ricky's here," she said.

"Good, maybe he can shed some light on this shit," said Ty.

Chapter Eighteen

Ty

Smiling faces sometimes pretend to be your friend. Smiling faces show no traces of the evil that lurks within. Smiling faces, smiling faces, sometimes they don't tell the truth. Smiling faces, smiling faces tell lies and I got proof.

—The Undisputed Truth, "Smiling Faces Sometimes"

Ty couldn't shake the feeling that something was off with Toni's story. It just seemed like too big of a coincidence. His mind kept replaying Maya's voice mail.

What the hell is going on? he thought.

"Hey, Ricky!" said Toni as she hugged him.

"Hey, lady! How are y'all doing?" asked Ricky, smiling and giving her flowers.

"Oh, these are gorgeous! Thank you so much. I love tulips, especially pink ones!" exclaimed Toni.

"It's the least I could do. I feel so bad about not being there for y'all. Your appointment is scheduled for 2:00 p.m. at Santa Fe Day Spa, and it's already paid for. Enjoy yourself," said Ricky, smiling.

"I definitely will. Thanks so much! Look who's here," said Toni, pointing to Ricky.

Ricky walked in slowly. His heart beating loudly. He knew that Ty and Toni heard it. He didn't know if seeing him would trigger Ty's memory.

"Hey, man. Come on in here," stated Ty.

"Man, are you all right? Damn, I'm sorry I wasn't able to help," stated Ricky, shaking Ty's hand.

"It's all good. Sit down and let's talk," said Ty.

"Well, do you guys need anything before I leave?" Toni asked, grabbing her phone and purse.

"My head is still hurting a little bit. Grab my prescription for me," stated Ty.

"Honey, it hasn't been long enough. You have to wait at least six hours. You know what…"

"Just give me the damn pills," stated Ty, interrupting Toni.

"Get them yourself!" yelled Toni. She slammed the door and sped out of the driveway.

Ricky was very concerned. He'd never witnessed Ty like this with Toni. "Are y'all all right, man? She was just looking out," said Ricky.

"We're good. I'm just in a lot of pain. I'm losing my mind, bruh. I don't know what happened to me or who did it. This shit is just fucked up!" Ty yelled, grabbing his head. He began telling Ricky what he knew so far.

Ricky sat there listening. He couldn't speak. His mind just kept recalling what had happened. His palms began to get sweaty. Ty went over what Toni had told him about him leaving work, her impromptu trip with Maya, and what Maya said she'd heard.

"Ricky, Ricky?" stated Ty.

"Huh, what?" Ricky asked.

"Did you hear me?" asked Ty.

"Umm, no, man. I'm sorry. What?" asked Ricky.

Ty looked at his friend strangely. Here he was almost killed, and he wasn't even paying attention. "I said, did Maya even call you? Did I call you? What's going on?" asked Ty.

"Man, I never spoke to Maya. I never spoke with or saw you either. Look, man, try to get you some rest. You're going to drive yourself crazy, and Toni too! Chill out. I'll be right back," stated Ricky as he headed for the door.

He knew with Ty's determination it would only be a matter of time before he remembered. He'd also forgotten about Maya's call. *What if Toni and Maya would have pulled up*? he thought as he reached into his trunk to grab the cooler filled with beer.

When Ricky returned, Ty was staring at the TV. He looked dazed and confused. Ricky knew it was now or never.

"All right, man. I got just what you need. Let me put these in the fridge," Ricky said, holding up the cooler to his friend. Ty just nodded and continued staring at the TV.

Ricky was so nervous. He almost dropped the bag filled with powder. He quickly popped the cap and poured in the drugs. All the while, Ty was none the wiser. After slightly shaking the can a little and making sure no traces were on the rim, Ricky brought the beer to Ty.

"Here, dude, this should calm your ass down a little," Ricky said handing Ty the beer.

"Thanks, Ricky! I need to apologize to Toni too. I have been way out of line with her. I'm just pissed off about the whole thing, and I feel like she's not really helping," said Ty.

Ricky didn't speak. He just sat there, watching and waiting, like a lion stalking its prey. Just as Ty was about to take a sip, the doorbell rang. Both men were startled.

"Are you expecting anyone?" asked Ricky.

"Not that I know of. You mind getting that for me?" asked Ty.

"Sure thing," said Ricky. He reluctantly went to the door, hoping that Ty would still take a long swallow of the beer.

It was Mrs. Carol. She was standing there holding two paper bags filled with groceries. Ricky didn't know what to do, so after exhaling, he opened the door.

"Hey, baby! Ty and Toni home?" asked Mrs. Carol.

"Hi, yes! Umm, come on in," said Ricky as he grabbed the bags. He was so pissed. He had a mind to kill Mrs. Carol right along with Ty.

"Hey, Ty! How are you doing, baby? Oh, no no no! I'm not your mama, but I know she would agree with me that you don't need no alcohol," said Mrs. Carol while grabbing the beer from Ty's hand.

"But Mrs. Carol..." said Ty.

"No buts. Now, I'm going to cook y'all a nice meal, and you're going to go get in the bed and rest," said Mrs. Carol, interrupting. She went in the kitchen and poured Ty's beer down the drain.

Ricky gasped. He walked back in the living room, feeling defeated. *What the fuck am I going to do now*? he thought. "Man, I'm going to get outta here and let you get some rest. Call me if you need anything," said Ricky.

"All right, man! Mrs. Carol is my other mama. We'll grab some drinks when all this shit is over. Thanks for stopping by," said Ty.

Ricky smiled and shut the door as Ty headed to bed. Mrs. Carol gathered the pots and pans she needed for her homemade chicken soup and corn bread muffins. She began humming one of her favorite hymns, "He's an On-Time God."

Chapter Nineteen

Ricky

"Old raggedy bitch! I should go back in there and kill her ass too! Damn, Steven is going to be so fucking disappointed!" yelled Ricky while pulling out of Ty's driveway. To say he was pissed would be an understatement.

He sped on to the freeway, swerving in and out of traffic. He didn't know where he was going. He pulled over at a gas station and called Steven.

Unfortunately, Steven never answered. He sat at the gas station, contemplating his next move. Part of him wanted to try again but he didn't have any more of the white powder. He knew that this was far from over.

"Ty is determined to remember what happened. I don't know what to do," stated Ricky as he began to sob.

He was ashamed of what he had been reduced to lately. His lies and deception were finally catching up to him. He'd lost his wife and now was about to lose his best friend. He couldn't even blame it all on Steven.

His eyes were puffy and red when he looked at himself in the visor mirror. This image made him think of the day Steven professed his love for Maya to him.

It had been about eight months after Steven and Maya had been dating. Ricky was seeing less and less of Steven. They would text often, but as far as seeing each other, that had been out of the question. Maya always seemed to have some event to attend. It was always something. Steven also started inviting her to all of the mixers he would have with his firm.

Ricky decided to ask Steven for some alone time. Once he agreed, the two met up in Atlanta. Steven had a conference up there, and Ricky took off from work a few days. This would be the first time the men didn't stay at the Hamilton.

They opted for the Courtyard Marriott right off of Peachtree in Buckhead. It wasn't far from the conference center. It also gave the men a nice change in scenery.

They enjoyed dinner at the Cheesecake Factory and did a little shopping at the Lennox Mall. Ricky noticed that Steven was kind of standoffish. He didn't have much to say and at times seemed as if he were ignoring Ricky.

"Are you okay?" asked Ricky as they stood in line for yogurt at the food court.

"I'm fine. Why do you ask?" asked Steven.

"Nothing, you just seem like you're in another world or something. Did I do anything to you to make you upset?" asked Ricky.

"My apologies. No, you haven't done anything to me. I just have a lot on my mind," stated Steven.

"Oh, you have a tough case coming up?" asked Ricky.

"No, it's nothing like that. I just have been thinking about Maya a lot lately. She's a great woman," stated Steven.

"You can't be serious. Maya is like the worst person I've ever met," laughed Ricky. "She literally lives to make Ty and Toni feel bad about themselves."

"Look, I know about all of that shit between them. To tell you the truth, they deserve every bit of it. Toni stole her man, for God's sake," stated Steven.

"Correction, Ty wasn't married, so technically he wasn't her man," clarified Ricky.

"Whatever, Toni was trifling as hell to fuck Ty. Don't act like you're the advocate for what's technical," stated Steven, feeling irritated with Ricky's statements about Maya.

Ricky stepped back from the line and walked away. His worst fears had finally presented themselves. He had the feeling that Steven was falling for Maya a few weeks ago. Now his blatant "taking up for her episode" proved it.

"Ricky, what's wrong with you, and where are you going?" asked Steven, catching up to him.

"What's wrong is that you're here with me but thinking about that bitch. That's what's wrong. She was only supposed to be a beard, Steven," stated Ricky.

"Oh, really? You get to go home to your wife while I get to go home to what? What do I get to go home to?" asked Steven.

"You're missing the point!" yelled Ricky.

"No, you're missing the point! The point is, I am no longer okay with being alone. I want someone in my life too. I love Maya. She's a great woman with a good head on her shoulders. You don't get to decide my life when you can't even fucking live yours!" yelled Steven.

The two men argued all the way back to their hotel. Ricky couldn't believe what he was hearing. Here he was risking it all for Steven, and Steven was planning a life with someone else.

Ricky cried with his back turned to Steven that night. He felt betrayed and secretly blamed Ty for making him introduce Maya and Steven. His life was falling apart, and there was absolutely nothing he could do about it.

After gathering his thoughts, Ricky pulled off. He let down his windows and blasted his radio. The only song that he wanted to hear was "You Wonder Why They Call You Bitch" by Tupac.

Chapter Twenty

Maya

*Bag lady, you gone hurt yo back draggin
all dem bags like that.*

—Erykah Badu, "Bag Lady"

Maya felt like a robot. Her thoughts were in a million pieces. She wasn't sure what was going on with Ty and Toni. She needed to get to the bottom of things, and fast. After getting herself together, she decided to call Toni.

"Toni, it's Maya. I'm not sure what's going on, but call me back when you get this," stated Maya to Toni's voice mail.

It was obvious that her best friend was ignoring her calls. She couldn't understand why. *It wasn't like I was going to answer my phone that early in the morning anyway. Hell, she knows how busy I am. Of course I'd be asleep at that hour*, she thought.

Maya grabbed her new Fendi purse and headed out the door. She figured she'd head to the chapel, finalize some things with her caterer, Maxine, and head to the

Santa Fe Day Spa for a quick facial. As she drove off, her focus shifted back to Ty.

Ty was the key to her happiness. She still loved him, but again he was standing in her way. This man had taken the place of her father. He assumed the responsibility of her heart and threw it away.

Now, she had to decide her next move. She thought about how Ty remembering would affect everyone. Everyone's lives lay in the balance of Ty remembering. She knew there would be no way to prove she knew what Steven did to Ty, but Steven would most definitely go to jail.

She almost hit the car in front of her while stopping at the red light. She was that deep in thought. She cringed at the thought of Toni seeing Steven arrested.

The chapel didn't seem as happy to her when she turned into the parking lot. She sat in her car, just looking at the chapel. Ty and Toni's wedding wasn't anywhere near as glamorous as hers would be, but the thought of it devastated her nonetheless. Her mind drifted to Toni's wedding day.

The courthouse was ten minutes away from the hotel Toni had stayed at the night before. Maya didn't want to even be in attendance. She was shocked at the absolute gall of Toni to ask her to be her maid of honor. Up until then, she had done a pretty decent job at keeping her love for Ty at bay.

She tried coming up with excuse after excuse, but Toni insisted that she needed her best friend by her side.

Reluctantly, Maya agreed. She hated Toni for making her witness the marriage, though.

Maya had to help Toni get dressed once she found out Toni's mother and stepdad were running late. She tried to smile and act as if she were happy for her friend. She had to appear to be, anyway.

Toni opted to wear a basic white dress with embroidered pearls around the front. She wore her hair in its signature bun. She wore a pair of white heels. Maya laughed to herself, thinking of how plain Toni was in comparison to her. She couldn't wrap her mind around why Ty would ever chose Toni.

Once they made it to the courthouse, she got her answer. Ty looked at Toni in a way he never looked at Maya before. His eyes lit up the moment she entered the room. Maya's only solace was the fact that Ty's mom was there, and she could see that his mom did not want him to marry Toni.

As Maya stood there, her heart felt as though she were conscious during open heart surgery. She could feel her chest being cracked open. She felt the incisions. She felt the pain.

Her eyes filled with tears. Tears she could no longer hold back. She wept.

She refused to look at Ty. She couldn't. If their eyes had met, he would have known that she wanted to be the one standing beside him.

When the two said their vows to each other, Maya drowned them out with thoughts of all the promises Ty had made to her. He told her that he had never met a woman as driven as she was. He told her that one day he was going to make her his bride, and she wouldn't have to want or worry about anything. She recalled bragging to Toni about it too.

After Toni and Ty were pronounced husband and wife, Maya forced herself to smile and clap along with everyone else. The smile remained fixed on her face the rest of the day. It was if she were wearing a mask. Underneath was a woman who was in deep sadness. She realized that ever since she'd caught Toni and Ty, the mask had already made itself as a permanent fixture in her life.

Maya gazed at the chapel as the memory fizzled out of her mind. She began to imagine June 17. She saw herself in her beautiful dress. She saw Steven kissing her and then the police pulling him away.

I can't allow Ty to ruin my life again, she thought as she walked toward the entrance.

Maya was happy that things were starting to fall in place despite the whole date mix-up. Even though she was in a chapel, she made sure to let them know how unhappy she was with the mix-up. They assured her that they would do everything they could to help accommodate anything she needed.

After finalizing the new wedding date, Maya called her caterer, Maxine. She knew it was short notice but hoped that she could get her to book the new date instead. Maxine agreed reluctantly. She had a wedding that afternoon and hated being booked twice on the same day. She liked to utilize her entire staff and not have to pay for extra help.

Maya called the spa and asked if they had any availability for her to get a mini facial. They told her yes, as long as she came right now. Maya smiled and began to relax a little bit.

"Now all I have to do is send out updated invitations and reschedule our flights and resort stay in the Cayman Islands. This wedding planning stuff is for the birds, but it'll be all worth it once I can officially add 'wife' to my list of accomplishments!" Maya stated as she turned on the interstate to head to the spa.

Chapter Twenty-One

Toni

*What about your friends? Will they stand
their ground? Will they let you down, again?
What about your friends? Are they gonna
be lowdown? Will they ever be around? Or
will they turn their backs on you?*

—TLC, "What about Your Friends"

The spa was so inviting. As Toni walked in, she instantly began to feel relaxed. The staff was always very friendly, and the aromatherapy candles created a luxurious ambiance. The smell always reminded Toni of the store Bath and Body Works.

After checking in, she headed for the steam shower. It relaxed her before and after her visits. Everything was very neat and super clean. She grabbed her pink plush robe and headed for the lounge area. There she was greeted with a complimentary bowl of fresh strawberries and a glass of pink moscato. *This is the perfect way to begin a spa day*, she thought.

After an amazing deep-tissue massage, Toni settled into a huge plush sofa in the lounge area. She found her favorite Pandora station and put in her ear buds. She had about twenty minutes before her facial.

She noticed a missed call and voice mail from Maya. She decided to decline calling back. She exhaled and closed her eyes. The last thing she wanted to do was hear Maya's lame-ass excuse. It was always something more important when it came to her. Toni was getting tired of the back and forth.

"Well, well, well! What do we have here?" said Maya pulling the ear buds out of Toni's ears.

"Maya, what are you doing here?" asked Toni, shocked as hell.

"What am I doing here? What the hell are you doing here when Ty is in the hospital?" asked Maya.

"First of all, Ty is at home, and secondly, if you would have bothered to answer your phone, you would have known that. Why are you here, knowing that my husband and your friend is in the hospital?" asked Toni, upset that Maya totally just killed her vibe.

"Excuse me? I lost my phone, and I called you the minute I found it and heard your voice mail," lied Maya matter of factly.

"Oh, really? You haven't even asked me if he is even okay," stated Toni.

"Toni, you're at the spa. Obviously, he's okay," stated Maya bluntly.

"That's beside the point, Maya. And he's far from okay," said Toni.

"Well, what happened?" asked Maya.

Toni took a deep breath. "Ty was on his way to see Ricky and ended up getting robbed before he got there, or at least that's what we think. They busted his head and left him in the trunk of his car, Maya." Toni held back her tears.

"Oh my God! I'm so sorry." Maya actually shocked herself. She really felt sorry for her friend. She even felt guilty for finding pleasure in Toni's pain. *So that's what Ricky and Steven were talking about. Maybe they saw what happened and didn't want to get involved*, she thought.

"Maya, it gets worse. He doesn't even know who did it. He doesn't even know what happened," stated Toni.

"Why not?" asked Maya, hoping Toni would tell her the same thing as the detectives had.

"He has short-term memory loss. The doctor said that he may or may not even remember. I'm so scared for him. I've never seen him like this," said Toni, feeling vulnerable.

"Short-term memory loss? Lord, have mercy. It's going to be okay, Toni. Do you need anything?" said Maya as she hugged her friend.

For a split second, Toni actually believed that her concern was genuine. She actually wanted to break down and cry in her best friend's arms. She wanted to tell her how scared she was for her husband. She wanted to reveal that she wasn't even happy in her marriage. She wanted to tell her that she had dreams and aspirations she wanted to accomplish. But the realization of where the two were even having the conversation brought her back to reality and made her pull away.

"What's wrong, Toni?" asked Maya.

"Maya, answer me one question. Just one," stated Toni.

"Okay, what is it?" asked Maya.

"When you heard the voice mail, did you get in your car and come to the hospital, or did you just wait for me to call you back?" asked Toni.

Maya just stood there. She couldn't answer. She wasn't sure how to answer that.

"Toni Weeks?" asked the esthetician, interrupting the awkward silence between the two women.

Toni didn't answer. She just collected her things and left Maya standing there. Toni couldn't believe Maya's response or lack thereof, but she was glad she'd posed the question to her. *A real friend would have gotten the message and come to the hospital regardless of a call back or not. Instead, this bitch is at the spa literally going on with her life as if nothing happened. Why the fuck do I keep dealing with her*? Toni thought as she was getting her facial.

With her skin feeling refreshed, Toni decided to call her daughter once she got in her car. She needed to hear her little voice. She missed her terribly. She took a deep breath and called Mildred.

"Hello," answered Mildred.

"Hi, Mildred, how are you all doing?" asked Toni.

"We are doing all right. Jessica is sleeping. How's my son?" asked Mildred, not concerned about Toni in the least.

"Oh, I wanted to talk to her. He's doing fine, I guess. I'm not home right now. He is at home with his friend Ricky," stated Toni, regretting her honesty.

"Well, where are you?" asked Mildred.

"Ricky decided to send me to the spa today. He thought I needed a break and a chance to relax after everything that has happened," stated Toni.

"Let me get this straight. *You* needed a break while at the hospital, and now *you* need another one?" asked Mildred.

"Yes, Mildred. You're absolutely correct. I needed a break," stated Toni, feeling her blood begin to boil.

"Well, I'll be. Child, if I needed as many breaks from life as you, I'd never get anything accomplished. Forgive me, but it's hard for me to believe that after everything *Ty* has been through, you are the one who needs a break," stated Mildred.

"Mildred, please call me when my daughter wakes up," stated Toni.

"Will do," stated Mildred, and she hung up.

Toni just sat there, glaring at her phone. She was so sick of having to deal with Ty's mom and her bullshit. She turned on the ignition and began to scroll through text messages.

After noticing three more texts from Benjamin, Toni decided to call him on her way home. She was feeling relaxed, upset, and confused all at the same time. She wasn't sure why she was even calling him, but she didn't have anyone to listen. The whole bullshit with Maya and her mother-in-law sent her into overdrive.

During their conversation, Benjamin told her he hated that she was going through so much. He sympathized with her situation and told her that Ty had to be the luckiest man on earth to survive such a terrible event. He also said that she was welcome to call him, if she ever needed to talk. Toni made a mental note of that. She knew she would never take him up on his offer, but it was still good to know. It was good to have someone there to listen, just in case.

Lord knew she couldn't call her mama. Their relationship had been strained over the years. It was mainly because of her step-dad. He always had something to say when Toni wanted to spend time with her mother. They hadn't spoken in weeks.

She never really spoke with her dad either. Last she'd heard, he had moved to Jersey with some building developing company. She exhaled as she realized she was completely alone.

Chapter Twenty-Two

Ty

The detectives arrived at Ricky's house after securing the search warrant. The goal was simple. All they had to do was find enough evidence to show that Ty had been there. Their first stop was the trash can. Detective Reed noticed that it had been moved to the front.

"Dammit! Are you fucking kidding me? It's trash day!" screamed Detective Price as he opened up what was now an empty trash can.

"Let's call for more back up and get inside. This son of a bitch thinks he's smart," stated Detective Reed.

Just then, they received a call from their lieutenant. He had reviewed the search warrant and found they had no probable cause to search the house. The detectives tried to explain their reasoning, but to no avail. The lieutenant had come under fire after a recent audit and was not going to take any chances on anything. His whole department was counting on him.

"Damn! Back to the drawing board," stated Detective Price as he drove off.

"Don't worry. We'll be back," stated Detective Reed.

"So what do you think about Miss Fisher?" asked Detective Price.

"I kind of got a feeling that she was hiding something. Honestly, she didn't seem that shocked. Did you notice how relieved she looked when we mentioned Mr. Weeks's short-term memory loss?" asked Detective Reed.

"I noticed that. I couldn't tell if she was relieved he was okay or relieved he didn't remember," stated Detective Price.

"Mr. Weeks received his warning around dusk. Then the officer stated that he turned around and went in the opposite direction of where he was going. What made him turn around?" asked Reed.

"That's the magic question. If we can answer that, I can guarantee you that we can solve this case. Whoever did that to him is an animal and needs to be locked the hell up. I mean seriously, they left the man to die in the trunk of his own fucking car. He has a wife and child at home. Imagine the conversation if he had been killed," said Detective Price.

"I don't even want to think about it. I've had enough of them to last me a lifetime," stated Detective Reed.

"Let's look a bit more into his relationship with Toni," stated Detective Price.

"Could you be a bit more specific?" asked Detective Reed.

"Life insurance? From what we know, she is not working. Maybe she got tired and wanted a clean break from him. Can we pull his insurance records?" asked Detective Price.

"You know, I really don't think it's his wife. She seemed genuinely concerned and forthcoming. I've seen lots of guilty people portray their innocence. She seems innocent to me. I think we are looking in the right area," stated Detective Reed.

"But why? I can't see a motive. Why would his best friend want him dead?" asked Detective Price.

"That, my friend, is why we are detectives. Let's head back to the station and figure this shit out," stated Detective Reed.

Chapter Twenty-Three

Ricky

Or do you not think so far ahead? Cause
I've been thinkin' 'bout forever.

—Frank Ocean, "Thinkin' 'Bout You"

Steven left in a hurry. Maya had thought that they were going to spend the entire day together. He told her he had some work to finish up at the office and would be tied up the entire day.

Steven was a mission, though. The revelation of Laila mentioning his involvement to Toni was the last straw. He knew it was only a matter of time before she violated the gag order. He'd already paid off her private investigator; now, his focus moved to Laila.

After several calls and Google searches, he figured out her address. He also knew that she would be getting off around five that evening. He gassed up his car and headed to Atlanta.

Once he found her apartment, he used his credit card in the door. It opened without any more effort. He slowly walked around Laila's apartment, checking to see if anyone else was there.

The apartment was empty. Steven let out a sigh of relief. He put on gloves, closed all of the curtains, and cut off the electricity. He noticed a closet near the front door. *This is a perfect spot*, he thought.

About thirty minutes later, Laila arrived. She opened the door and tried to put on her lights. She flicked them over and over.

"What is going on? I know damn well I paid the bill. And didn't I open those curtains," she stated as she closed the door.

As soon as Steven heard the door lock, he eased out of the closet and grabbed Laila around her mouth.

"Shhh, be quiet. I promise it won't hurt," said Steven. Laila tried to scream, but to no avail. Steven pulled her down and choked her to death.

Once he was sure she was dead, he put the electricity back on. He placed a bedsheet around her neck and hung her from the rafter above her bedroom closet. He placed a suicide note on her pillow and left.

She got what she deserved. If she had just kept her damn mouth shut, she would still be alive. She knew too much. No one is going to stop me from having what I want. I know how women are. She would tell Toni, and

K. Reshay

that would be the end of me and Maya. I can't let that happen. I love her, he thought as he drove off.

After Steven made it back to Birmingham, he put his cell back on. He had voice mails from Ricky and Maya. He decided to call Ricky first.

"Man, where the fuck have you been? I've been trying to reach you for hours!" yelled Ricky.

"First off, why the fuck are you yelling?" asked Steven calmly.

"I just told you why. Look, where are you? I've been hanging around Birmingham all this fucking time," stated Ricky.

Sensing Ricky was all torn up over killing Ty, Steven quickly jolted back to attorney mode.

"We shouldn't talk over the phone. Meet me at my place. I'll be there shortly," stated Steven.

With that, he hung up the phone. After waiting a few minutes, he called Maya. "Hey, baby!" exclaimed Steven.

"*Hey, baby?* Steven, what's going on? I've been calling you for hours," stated Maya. Steven could hear the tension in her voice.

"Calm down, will you? I told you I had to work today. Where is all of this coming from?" asked Steven.

"It's coming from someone who is tired. I'm tired of not being able to reach you," said Maya with lots of attitude.

"Well, get used to it because I'm a lawyer and a damn good one. I can't always be at your beck and call," stated Steven as he pulled into his garage.

114

Maya quickly changed her tone. The last thing she needed was Steven to be mad at her.

"All I'm saying is that I worry about you. Anyway, how about dinner tonight? I was thinking about making that rosemary chicken you like so much with asparagus and whipped potatoes," stated Maya.

"As much as I would like to, I can't. I'm still swamped with work. I'll probably eat some leftover takeout or something," said Steven, hoping she'd get the hint.

"Well, I can always just cook it and bring it over for you," stated Maya.

"Maya, I'm really busy tonight. How about you wait and cook it tomorrow," stated Steven.

"Fine, Steven. Talk to you tomorrow," stated Maya. She didn't even wait for Steven to respond. She just hung up.

Steven headed inside, not giving Maya's conversation a second thought. He was just elated that he had gotten rid of Laila and that Ricky had gotten rid of Ty. He was ready to celebrate in their victory. He knew that once Maya found out about Ty's death that he would have to console her for a few days, so he needed this night with Ricky.

He quickly showered and lit candles. He put on John Coltrane's "My Shining Hour" and poured two glasses of wine. Her rambled around in his fridge, trying to figure out what he could make for dinner. He finally settled on salmon with his special glaze and roasted veggies. The mood was set. All he needed was his Ricky.

Chapter Twenty-Four

Maya

Maya realized that Steven wasn't going to call her back. She actually held her phone for minutes, just staring at the screen. She decided that he was just stressed out and decided to cook his favorite meal anyway.

She went about the kitchen, grabbing all of the ingredients. She began washing and seasoning the chicken. She washed and cut up the potatoes. She even began roasting the asparagus. Just when she was about to put the chicken in the oven, she threw the entire dish into her sink, shattering glass everywhere.

"Why am I even cooking for this bastard? He isn't going to come over! He doesn't want me to come over!" Maya yelled. Her frustration with her situation was boiling over.

After turning off the stove, she poured herself a glass of wine and went out on her balcony without even cleaning up. The night air was cool. The stars shone brightly as a gentle breeze dried the sweat on Maya's face. Somehow, it managed to calm her down.

She had thoughts of Toni. Their conversation had been short but intense all the same. She wondered if the tables were turned, would Toni drive to the hospital for her and her husband.

She caught herself in midponder because she already knew the answer. Toni would have driven to that hospital as soon as she got the call. Despite what happened years ago, Toni still was her friend. She remembered how coldly she'd treated Toni when she told her she was pregnant.

Maya had recently bought her new Mercedes and was so excited to show Toni. She didn't want to tell her she was getting one. She just wanted to see the surprised look on her face.

After getting her makeup done at the Mac counter at the Galleria mall, Maya called Toni. "Hey, girl! What are you doing today?" asked Maya.

"Hey, nothing much. I need to finish ironing clothes, but that's it," stated Toni.

"Okay, let's go to lunch. I've been dying to try this chicken noodle bowl from Surin West. My client eats there all the time and suggested that I try it," stated Maya.

"I'm not really feeling up to eating right now," stated Toni.

"You'll be okay, girl. Tell you what, I'll come pick you up in about an hour," stated Maya. Toni reluctantly agreed.

Maya figured that an hour would be enough time for her to find a cute outfit to match her new ride. *Fresh new look, new outfit, and a new ride*, she thought.

She decided on a pair of jeans, something she rarely wore, and a cute pink shirt. She found some beige

Jessica Simpson heels from Belk and decided to buy a new Michael Kors purse to match while she was at it.

She looked good and knew that she would feel even better once she shoved her new car down Toni's throat. She pulled out of the mall feeling like a million bucks. She texted Toni that she was on her way.

Once she got there, Maya blew her horn several times. Toni took forever to come out. Maya couldn't even contain her excitement. She stepped out of the car and leaned against it once she saw the front door open.

"Oh my God! Maya, this car is hot!" exclaimed Toni as she walked out. Maya noticed how pretty Toni was that day. Her beauty was effortless. All she had on was a maxi shirt and tank top, and she still was gorgeous.

"Thanks, lady! I figured I'd treat myself to a little something in the 60k range. Nothing fancy but, hey, you only live once," she stated as she hugged her friend.

"Well, this car is too cute. I'm so happy for you, Maya," stated Toni as she sat in the passenger seat.

Maya played her favorite Beyonce songs as she bragged about the cost of her vehicle and all of its bells and whistles. She noticed that Toni wasn't as excited as she would have liked her to be. She simply thought that Toni was trying to hide her jealousy.

Once they arrived at the restaurant, Maya's bragging continued. "So you know that I sold the Jenkins house, right?" she asked.

"No, I didn't, but I'm glad you did. I stayed over there for four hours getting that place ready for your open house," laughed Toni.

"Well, it's not like you have anything else to do. Anyway, I made like ten grand in commission. So I was like, let me do something for myself," stated Maya.

She noticed that Toni didn't look so good. "I'll be right back," stated Toni as she left the table.

Maya sat there, relishing in her accomplishments. She was so excited about the day. Here she was, looking pretty and with a new car to boot. She felt like everything was coming together for her. She knew that even though Toni would never admit it, she definitely was jealous.

A few minutes later, Toni came back to the table. Her face was flushed. She asked for a ginger ale and wiped her face with her napkin.

"Are you okay?" asked Maya, knowing that she wasn't. She knew that her friend had just been bitten by the green bug of envy.

"Actually, I'm not okay. Well, I guess I am okay. It's not the end of the world or nothing," stated Toni.

"Well, what is it?" asked Maya as she took another bite out of her chicken noodle bowl.

"I'm pregnant, Maya," stated Toni.

"You're what? Toni, are you serious?" asked Maya. The food was now stuck in her throat. She was unable to swallow. Her forehead frowned.

"I'm pregnant." Toni smiled.

"How far along?" asked Maya, putting her napkin in her bowl. She no longer had an appetite.

"I am about two months. I just found out the other day," said Toni as she thanked the server for her ginger ale.

"Well, I'll be. How in the world are you all going to afford a baby, Toni?" asked Maya.

"The word is 'congratulations,' Maya," stated Toni, ignoring her comment.

"Yes, congrats, but how are y'all going to afford a baby on Ty's salary?" asked Maya.

"I don't know, but he'll make a way. Ty told me to let him worry about that. He told me to just relax and take care of his baby," stated Toni, sipping her drink.

"Excuse me for a moment, girl. I need to use the restroom," stated Maya. Once she went in the stall, she began to cry. She tried her best to hold it in, but she simply couldn't. Her whole day had revolved around making Toni jealous of her. Jealous of her money and of her success, not to mention her new car. And just like that, Toni managed to ruin her day with the news of a baby.

She'd once told Ty during a lovemaking session that she wanted to have his baby. He told her that he loved her and that he would give her a baby. Now, Toni was giving him the one thing she wanted.

She dried her face and barely said two words to Toni. She hurried up and took her home and didn't speak to her for weeks. Every time Toni would call, she would ignore her or text back that she was busy with a client or something. She felt betrayed all over again.

Maya realized that the fact she had held on to Toni's betrayal after all these years was truly mind blowing. She knew that Toni still felt guilty. She still loved Ty, so she considered it well-deserved guilt.

Then her mind drifted back to Steven. He certainly rushed her off the phone. *Why was he acting funny*? she thought, gulping down glass two of her wine.

She recalled the night she heard Steven yell at Ricky. It was obvious that this was around the same time Ty was supposed to be over at Ricky's house. The rage in Steven's voice proved that it must have been some sort of argument or something.

What she couldn't figure out was why. She couldn't possibly even remember a time when the two even argued. *What happened to make them turn on Ty, for God's sake*? she thought.

She was glad she'd brought the entire wine bottle with her. After pouring another glass, she looked around her balcony. Not even a good twenty-four hours ago, she was fucking her man and reveling in Toni's misery. Now, she was alone, trying to get things the fuck off her mind.

The night sky was so serene. She got up and stumbled to her balcony's edge and looked down to the street below. *I should just end it all it all right now. I could just be done with all of this hurting. I don't even know why I'm even in existence. Even if I marry Steven, I'll always wonder about him. What if he really is gay? Why can't I just be happy?* she thought.

Ending it all was out of the question once she realized that she couldn't win if she were dead. She made her warped mind rationalize that the only way to really win was to stick to her plan of becoming the wife of a prestigious attorney and live in a beautiful home.

This revelation gave Maya an idea. She stumbled inside and went to her gorgeous white-and-gold armoire. She pulled out her black Victoria's Secret lace lingerie with the G-string. *I just may wear this for Steven tonight*, she thought. She grabbed it along with her keys and headed out the door.

Chapter Twenty-Five

Toni

Tell me why I'm living, some days my work seems so in vain. I talk to you, you don't hear nothing I say. What's up with this game? Why am I so forgiving?

—Chrisette Michele, "Goodbye Game"

The suds had already left the water as Toni continued to stare at the dishes. Her mind was all over the place. After returning home, she was in yet another argument with Ty.

She didn't even understand the argument. He was just agitated about not getting answers from Ricky. All she knew was that the more she tried to reason with him, the angrier he became.

She decided to clean up after he stormed out back with a beer. A beer he knew he shouldn't be drinking per her conversation with Mrs. Carol.

She was so tired. All of the stress removed from her earlier today had been quickly placed back during her encounter with Maya. Now, another argument with Ty. And to top it all off, her baby was miles away from her with a woman who hated Toni.

Her sadness turned to anger. She was angry at Ty, angry at Maya, and had had enough of her mother-in-law. It was getting to be way too much.

"Fuck these dishes!" she yelled.

She dried her hands, grabbed her purse, and headed out the door. She didn't know where she was going, but she knew she needed to get out of there to clear her head. She blasted her radio and drove, secretly wishing she had a girlfriend to meet up with for drinks. As much as she wanted to dial her number, she knew Maya wouldn't offer any support.

After their conversation at the spa, she wondered if there would even be a friendship. She remained annoyed at the fact that Maya only called her and left a message. *I don't even know why I was surprised. Maya has never been right since the whole Ty mess*, she thought.

Laila came to mind. She grabbed her phone to call her but noticed that Benjamin was calling.

"Umm, hello?" asked Toni, puzzled as to why he was calling when he knew that she was married.

"Toni, I'm sorry for calling you, but didn't I just pass you?" asked Benjamin.

"Pass me? I don't think so. Where are you?" asked Toni.

"I'm heading toward downtown and looks like you're headed toward Hoover," he stated.

"Well, guess you did see me then. Any who, what's up?" she asked.

"I should be asking you that. Why are you out so late? Where are you heading?" asked Benjamin.

"I'm just out and about. I needed to clear my head," Toni stated.

"Toni, you should not have to leave home to clear your head. I don't live too far. Would you like to just chill at my place? I'd feel better if you weren't out alone," he stated.

Toni paused. She knew damn well that going to Ben's house would be a bad idea. She'd never even thought about another man's company since she'd been with Ty.

"Toni, are you still there?" asked Benjamin.

"I'm here. Sorry, I really don't think that would be a good idea. I just want to ride a bit," stated Toni.

That comment made Benjamin's dick hard. He rubbed it and imagined Toni doing just that. She was so damn sexy to him.

"Listen, I will just let you inside. I'll leave. I just want you to be okay. You really don't need to be driving out late like this. It's dangerous," he stated.

"Thanks for the concern, but I can't ask you to leave me at your house. I'll be fine," stated Toni, bravely fighting temptation.

"Toni, where are you now?" asked Benjamin.

"I'm passing the Galleria mall," she stated.

"Well, pull over at that Steak 'n Shake on your left. I'm on my way," he stated.

"But..." stated Toni.

Benjamin had already hung up. She wasn't sure what to do at that point, but she did know that she didn't want to drive all night. She also knew that she wasn't ready to go back home. So she pulled over and waited for her new source of comfort.

Chapter Twenty-Six

Ty

When a woman's fed up, it ain't nothin'
you can do about it. It's like running out of
love. And then it's too late to talk about it.

—R. Kelly, "When a Woman's Fed Up"

Once Ty realized Toni had left, he became furious. His head began hurting again, so he grabbed some more of his prescription pills, this time taking two instead of one.

He couldn't even understand why she'd left. Her attitude had definitely changed. Usually, she didn't say much. He actually took advantage of that often. He noticed that the more successful Maya became, the more subservient Toni would become. She would go above and beyond making sure home life was perfect for him. He didn't mind that a bit.

He remembered when Maya was awarded sales consultant of the year. Her company was going to honor her at a celebration at the Ross Bridge Resort and Spa. Of course, she had invited them both.

Toni took weeks to decide on the perfect dresses for her and Jessica. She also had to find the perfect gift. Even though it put them back a bit, she settled on paying for a full spa day at Ross Bridge for Maya. Ty definitely didn't understand why her gift had to be so extravagant. He thought that flowers and a card would be enough.

Toni made sure that she made love to him the entire week before the event. She cooked all of his favorite meals that week too. He remembered coming home from work and trying to hide his grin as Toni cooked in his favorite dress.

The night before the event, Toni wore a pink teddy with lace trim for him. She fucked and sucked him all night long. Ty thought that he would be too tired to function the next day. One thing he knew for sure was that he was always fully sexually satisfied anytime Toni knew Maya would be around.

The day of the event, Toni went to go get her hair and nails done. She was so excited for Maya, but Ty could tell that she wanted to be the eye candy on his arm. He remembered how beautiful Toni and Jessica looked that night.

When Maya saw them, she was overly ecstatic. Maya and Steven had just started dating and looked very comfortable together. Maya received her award and thanked everyone. She even thanked the damn people who allowed her to cater luncheons at restaurants. She thanked everyone but her best friend. The one who practically pounded the payment for her passing out business cards and fliers. Toni alone had referred close to twenty-five clients to Maya, all of whom closed on houses. Not to mention, she helped her host luncheons and even helped her set up for open houses. Ty saw the disappointment on Toni's face.

During the dinner, Maya didn't even sit with them. She opted to sit with Steven and some of his business associates. Ty was so pissed. He told Toni that he wanted to leave before the dessert even came out, but Toni refused. After dinner, they walked over to Maya's table, and Jessica gave her a gorgeous bouquet of pink roses along with her gift card. Maya took the gift, said thank you, and continued on with her conversation as if they were her fans or something.

Once they left, Ty laid in to Toni. "Don't ask me to go to nothing else for Maya. I am so serious. This will be my last time. I have better things to do than support your so-called friend," stated Ty.

"Ty, she just had a lot going on. She had her boss there and potential clients. I'm sure she was just networking," stated Toni, trying to take up for her friend.

"Bullshit! I don't give a damn who was there or what she was trying to do, Toni. She blatantly ignored us. Then she thanks everyone but you! That is totally unacceptable," said Ty as he turned on to the interstate.

"She probably just forgot, Ty. It's not a big deal," stated Toni.

"Well, you sure as hell made it a big deal. And how could she forget you but remember to thank folks at restaurants? You've been talking about this for weeks. I know that you were disappointed. I could see it in your face. You helped her get that award. How many nights was my dinner late because you had to help Maya? And she couldn't even thank you?" asked Ty.

"Ty, just drop it, please. I wasn't looking for a thank you," stated Toni.

"No, I will not drop it, Toni. We just spent close to a grand trying to be there for your so-called best friend. The gift card you told me to get was around $350. You include that with your hair, those dresses, not to mention this damn tux you insisted I rent, and she can't even acknowledge you. Some. Damn. Friend," said Ty.

He and Toni argued the rest of the way home. He felt sorry for his wife but was also tired of her making excuses for Maya. He wanted to lay the shit out for her in black and white. He provided example after example, but Toni refused to admit that Maya was no good.

Deep down, Ty knew why, though. He knew that Toni still felt guilty for being with him. He also would never take responsibility for his part in it all, which was why he used her guilt to his advantage.

After warming up some more chicken soup, he decided to call his wife. She didn't answer. He called again. This time, Toni's phone went straight to voice mail.

"Look, I'm trying to see where you are. Call me back. This is ridiculous, Toni," he stated.

He started to call Maya but decided against it. He figured that Toni had just gone out for a drive or something.

He didn't feel bad about their argument, though. He felt like she really was not trying to help him.

The medicine started to take effect. The throbbing in his head began to subside. He was glad he had Mrs. Carol's soup. It somehow gave his body the nourishment no medicine could provide.

He showered and grabbed a piece of paper to jot down the time line of events. He was sure that something there would jog his memory.

"Let's see now. I left work early and was supposed to head to Ricky's house. But Ricky said that I never made it. He also said that he never talked to me. I wonder if I stopped or something?" Ty asked himself as he grabbed another beer from the fridge.

"Did I have a flat tire? Did I need some gas? Damn, I need to pull up my bank record, pull my cell phone record, and figure out what the fuck happened!" he yelled.

He placed his head in his hands. "Ricky didn't seem helpful. Toni is gone. What the fuck is happening to me?" he asked himself as he gulped his beer.

Chapter Twenty-Seven

Ricky

As now can't reveal the mystery of tomorrow. But in passing will grow older every day. Just as all is born is new, do know what I say is true, that I'll be loving you always.

—Stevie Wonder, "As"

Ricky didn't want to face Steven once he pulled up. He didn't seem to have the courage. The night air held so much mystery. He wanted to just remain outside. His mind created all kinds of scenarios that he could make up. He knew that Steven wouldn't buy the whole Mrs. Carol thing. It was crazy to him that the truth seemed so unbelievable.

He felt like such a failure. He had no real love life, and the one person that he considered being his best friend would have to die. He couldn't make himself understand why he'd even agreed to kill Ty. The only thing he could come up with was his own selfishness. He knew that if he called the police, Ty would have Steven arrested. Ty would probably tell everyone what he saw. It was bad enough that Laila knew.

Nevertheless, he loved his friend. Ty had been there for him through some really tough times. He had a family. He knew that Ty didn't deserve what had happened to him or what was going to happen.

When they were still in college, Ty helped Ricky. Ricky slept on Ty's couch for free and even ate for free most of the time. He had messed up his scholarship money on some pyramid scheme, and Ty practically carried him the whole year.

The next year, while still in college, Ricky finally got back up on his feet. He immediately went to Ty and offered him money, but Ty told him that it was fine.

"Man, look, we all go through stuff. I may need you one day. I didn't hold you down because I wanted you to repay me. I did it because we are boys," stated Ty.

Ricky just remembered thinking that he had never met a friend like Ty. He had never really been friends with someone as genuine as Ty. Anytime he needed something, Ty was right there for him. The same went for Ty as well. He would come to Ricky when he needed to be fronted a little cash. They were just like brothers.

Now, here he was trying to kill his friend not once but twice. He didn't even know how he was going to live with himself after all of this shit was said and done. Ty just had been at the wrong place at the wrong time. He knew too much and because of that, he was going to have to die.

Ricky stayed in his car as long as he could. He finally got out and headed for the wrath of Steven. Ricky exhaled deeply.

Steven didn't even give Ricky time to knock on the door. He opened it and invited his lover inside. He kissed him passionately.

"Steven, we have to talk," managed Ricky in between kisses.

"We can talk later. Come here. I want to show you something," stated Steven. He was only wearing a towel. He slowly undressed Ricky right at the door.

He led Ricky into his master bathroom. The smooth melodies of Coltrane played in the background. Candles were lit around the bubble-filled tub, and the aroma of Glade's Clean Linen filled the room.

Ricky couldn't speak. He saw that his lover had gone through so much trouble. He couldn't bring himself to ruin the mood, so he just went with the flow. *Might as well get laid first*, he thought.

The two men sat in the tub and began kissing. Ricky looked around the bathroom, and Steven immediately grabbed the blunt he'd rolled for his lover. The two men smoked the herb and blew shotguns into each other's mouths.

As their high took effect, Steven poured wine. The mood was filled with anticipation. Steven began rubbing Ricky's dick until it grew hard.

The wine and weed took over as Steven lowered his head under the water. He found Ricky's dick and took it in his mouth. He'd suck, come up for air, and do it again. He kept giving Ricky underwater head until he came.

Ricky was in complete sexual bliss as he began to kiss Steven. The passion between them was unreal. As the candles danced, so did the two bodies of the men. Their bodies intertwined to the sounds of the jazz playing softly in the background. Ricky's moans grew louder.

They made love until the water turned cold in the tub. After drying off, they ate dinner and began kissing once more. The kissing led to another round of lovemaking. This time they ended up in Steven's king-size bed.

Steven knew he could never let Ricky go. They shared too many secrets. Of course, he'd never tell about what he did to Laila, but other truths between the two would remain.

After round two in Steven's bed was over, the two men lay still as they came down from their high. Their bodies relaxed from extreme sexual gratification. Steven relished in their victories.

There in the silence, Ricky finally spoke. "Steven, Ty is not dead."

Chapter Twenty-Eight

Maya

I believe I'll go back home and start all over again. I left my rainbow behind me, right where I began.

—Mckinley Mitchell, "The End of the Rainbow"

Wiping away tears, Maya pulled into the Pemberbrook Commons subdivision. She really needed to get herself together. Lights were on in many homes. She marveled at the neighborhood's superb beauty.

She pulled into the driveway of her new home. The outside was absolutely gorgeous. She especially liked its long entrance to get there and circular driveway.

All of the lights were on to keep would-be burglars away. She grabbed her realtor's key and let herself inside. The home smelled like money. Anyone entering it would definitely feel as if he or she had made it.

There was a huge chandelier that hung in the entryway. It sparkled as the lights hit it. There also were two large white columns on each side of the foyer. Maya pulled out her home design magazine from her purse and envisioned how her new home would eventually look.

She walked throughout the home and gazed in the doorways of each room. She imagined being carried over the threshold. She could see the dinner parties she'd host for Steven's prestigious associates and clients. She could see the Christmas decorations throughout her new home. She closed her eyes and imagined kids coming down the stairs, running toward their huge Christmas tree for Santa's gifts.

She saw holiday parties, happiness, and peace. She opened her eyes back to the empty home. *It certainly has potential*, she thought.

She grabbed the overnight bag she kept in her car and showered in the master bath. She imagined Ty waiting for her. She wanted Ty to be waiting for her but knew that the days for that were pretty much over. After drying off, she put on the lingerie she'd brought along with her trench coat. She wanted to surprise the man she did have.

"The memories we would create here would be divine. Toni would never admit it, but she'd be jealous of my new life. It will be perfect. I'll see to it," Maya stated as she locked the door.

Visiting her new home certainly made her feel better. She pulled out of the driveway and called Steven. She knew it was late, but she was hoping he would answer.

She wanted to pick him up and bring him back to Pemberbrook. She wanted him to see their new home again. She wanted him to fuck her in every room. She needed him inside her again. There was no way she'd be able to sleep tonight unless he was inside of her.

After several rings and unanswered texts, she figured he was asleep. *No biggie. I'll just go by there and let myself inside. I can make love to him all night, and then I'll let him fuck me all over our new house tomorrow*, she thought.

She could feel her pussy throb with anticipation the closer she got to Steven's house. She called one last time, hoping he would answer so they could actually do part A of her plan. As she turned on to the street, she noticed Ricky's car in the driveway. *What the fuck*? she thought.

"I can't believe this shit! This motherfucker has Ricky over here and not me. No wonder his ass rushed me off the phone," she stated as she pulled near the driveway and turned off her ignition.

She prepared herself for the worst as she stormed out. She grabbed the spare key and let herself inside slowly, hoping the two men didn't hear her. She decided not to close the door. Once inside, she noticed men's clothes on the floor, saw the faint lights of candles, and heard jazz playing. Her heart sank. She stopped dead in her tracks.

If I go any further, my relationship will be over, she thought. She couldn't face the truth even though it was staring her in her face. Wanting to keep up with appearances made her want to remain blind to the obvious. She slowly closed the door, put back the spare key, and ran to her car as fast as she could. Her heart was pounding, and beads of sweat surfaced under her arms and on her forehead.

"Fuck! Fuck!" she screamed as she hit her hands on the steering wheel. "I will not let Ricky have my man! I fucking refuse to accept this shit! I cannot! No, I will not lose my chance at happiness. I'm too close. Too fucking close to having everything I've ever wanted. I have to figure out how to stop Ty from remembering and how to get Ricky the fuck out of the picture. I'll do whatever I have to! Whatever. I. Have. To."

Chapter Twenty-Nine

Toni

*I can't hold it in forever. Eventually, I'd
have to breathe. Done hid a lot behind
the light, behind the wall. Now, it's crashing in on me.*

*—Jill Scott, "Comes to the Light
(Everything)"*

Benjamin's house was located right off of the Lorna Road exit
in Hoover. It was in a nice neighborhood. Toni remembered
dropping Gloria off there when her car was in the shop.

Benjamin motioned for Toni to pull into his garage.
Although she thought that was a bit odd, she did. His car
remained parked in the driveway. He gave her his garage
opener as they walked inside.

"Come on in and make yourself at home. Are you hun-
gry?" he asked.

"Umm, no, I'm fine," stated Toni as she admired his
huge aquarium filled with what looked like exotic fish. She

kept her arms folded as she continued to look at her surroundings. The living area had huge leather furniture and a large screen t.v. There were several African animal paintings on the walls. The decor had a safari type of feel to it.

"Okay, can I get you something to drink? I have juice, water, soda," he stated.

Toni interrupted. "You know, I could use some wine. Do you have any?"

"Yes, I have some white wine," he stated. He grabbed the wine opener and washed one glass. He poured the wine and brought it to her.

"Thanks. I must say this is a nice place you have here," stated Toni after taking a sip.

"Well, I can't take all of the credit. Gloria took one look at this place a few months after I moved in, and the rest is history." He laughed.

"Yes, Gloria does have great taste. I definitely can see it now that you've mentioned it," stated Toni.

"Wait a minute, now. I did pick out the rug and the bar stools over there," laughed Ben.

"Oh yeah, they are all right. I can tell that Gloria didn't pick those too!" she joked.

"I see you got jokes. It's okay, though. Well, have a seat and relax. Here's the remote, and you have the garage opener. The bathroom is on the right down the hall, and feel free to grab whatever you'd like out of the fridge," instructed Benjamin.

"Are you leaving me here by myself?" asked Toni.

"Yeah, I don't want to make you uncomfortable or anything. Plus, I was headed out, anyway," he stated.

"Actually, I could use some company. I never have anyone to really talk to," stated Toni. The last thing she wanted to be right now was alone.

"In that case, let me pour me some wine, and we can talk," said Benjamin.

Toni made herself more comfortable. The wine managed to relax her enough to not care about the fact that she shouldn't even have her ass over here in the first place. She exhaled as she began to relay the events of her argument.

Benjamin listened to her, which was strange to Toni because she was so used to being interrupted. He was a gentleman. He offered her the one thing she wasn't getting, which was genuine attention.

"Oh, wow! I've talked your ear off. My apologies. I didn't realize I had so much to say," stated Toni, feeling somewhat embarrassed.

"You have nothing to apologize for, Toni. I think you've done all you can give the situation. I can definitely understand Ty's frustration, but it isn't right to take it out on you. You can't make him remember what his mind has blocked out. Like the doctor said, it just takes time," stated Benjamin as he polished off the last of his wine. They had finished the entire bottle.

"You're right. It's getting late. I've taken up your whole night," stated Toni as she rose to leave.

"The pleasure has been all mine. I always enjoy the company of a beautiful woman." He smiled.

He rose to take the wine bottle into the kitchen, hoping she wouldn't notice the bulge in his jeans. He had been fighting the urge to make a move on her all night but couldn't prevent his arousal. He tried to put the wine bottle in front of it.

Toni blushed as she tried to ignore the obvious. Her pussy tingled as she pretended to be interested in the show on TV. She felt her panties get wet.

Benjamin came back from the kitchen. He had noticed her looking at his bulge when he got up. He could feel her body calling out to him.

"Thanks for the wine and conversation, Ben. I feel a little better," Toni stated as they made it to the garage.

Suddenly, Benjamin grabbed her arm and pulled her to him. He kissed her passionately. Toni fought back at first, but the more she fought, the tighter his grip became. She was trapped in his arms of seduction.

He slid his hand under her sundress in search for her creamy middle. He figured if she wasn't wet, he'd back off, apologize, and blame it on the wine. But just as he'd suspected, her panties were soaking wet. He slid them aside and stuck one of his fingers inside of her.

Toni moaned as he touched her. He never let go of her mouth with his tongue. He pulled his fingers out and sucked her juices from them. She tasted good. This turned Toni on even more. She grabbed his dick and pulled it out. It was extremely long and thick. Benjamin ripped her panties off and picked her up.

He placed her on the hood of her car and put her legs over his shoulders. He slid in her wet, throbbing pussy with ease. Toni gasped from the extreme width of his dick. His strokes were deep and fast. Toni's moans began to match his. It was good. Benjamin began trailing his tongue all over Toni's body, never losing the rhythm of his stroke. This man was taking her to a place she'd never been before.

Not wanting to come too fast, Benjamin pulled out and pushed Toni higher on the hood. He let his tongue take over. He started at her top lips and ended at her bottom lips. He dove in head first, licking every inch of her. His long tongue searched for the cream to come out. She felt it twirl inside of her. It reminded her of her vibrator. Benjamin made up in his mind that she was not leaving until he gave her at least three.

Toni screamed in ecstasy as she came. Her eyes rolled to the back of her head as Benjamin turned her over and began trailing his tongue back and forth to both holes. Satisfied that he had her leaking even more, he pulled her down and slipped in once again.

Toni couldn't control herself. His dick penetrated every crevice in her cunt. Her feet literally left the ground as he gripped her ass, fucking her harder from the back. She exploded once again. *That makes two*, thought Benjamin.

He pulled out, turned Toni around, and opened her car door. His dick bounced up and down as he walked. He pulled Toni onto his dick as he lay in the driver's seat. He gently released the pink pin holding Toni's hair in place, causing her silky long hair to fall in her face and onto her shoulders. He pulled out Toni's breasts to watch them bounce up and down. When he could no longer stand it, he grabbed them and started slurping on them loudly. Her nipples were so erect that they were extra sensitive.

Toni bounced up and down on Benjamin's dick. Having her hair down made her feel extra sexy as she rode. The dick was good. This man was fucking her properly. He allowed her to come again before he finally did. They tongue kissed each other passionately for minutes. They both tried to catch their breath. Their undeniable chemistry commanded attention.

He moaned in her ear, "I need you again, but this time in the shower."

Toni softly moaned, "Okay."

Chapter Thirty

Ty

Just because, I raise a little sand. I might be tired lady. Try to understand that doesn't mean that you've done something wrong. And just because when we have a little fight and I walk out the door and stay gone all night it doesn't mean that I won't be coming home. I love you. I love you. What else can I do or say?

—Johnnie Taylor, "Just Because"

Ty called Toni over and over again. He was getting more and more pissed by the hour. It was after midnight. He paced back and forth, trying to calm himself down. He forced himself to believe the argument was all of Toni's fault. *She wasn't even trying to help me remember what the fuck happened to me*, he thought.

After stepping outside, the darkness frightened him. It was a familiar darkness that he usually didn't get when the lights were out. It felt as if he'd been in this type of complete darkness before, but it wasn't caused by being outside. He shuddered at the thought of what could have happened to him. He feared what could possibly happen to his family.

"These motherfuckers have my wallet! They know where I live and where I work, and they even have all my shit out of my car. They have pictures of my family too. What the fuck am I going to do? The fucking detectives didn't mention anything about protection or nothing. Hell, we should be in protective custody. At least until those bastards are caught," stated Ty.

His heart skipped a beat when he saw a car in the distance. He figured it was Toni, but it ended up not being her. *Hell, what if they find out that I'm not dead. They'll think I'm a fucking witness or something. They won't know that I don't remember what happened*, he thought.

This realization wanted him to keep Jessica at his parents' house even longer. It also made him even more frustrated with Toni. They had argued so much that they haven't even taken the time to discuss their safety.

"I don't give a fuck how mad she is! She should have better sense than to be out this time of night knowing my mental state," he stated as he closed the front door.

He went back to his time line of events. He figured that instead of focusing on what he didn't remember, he should start to focus on what he did. He knew that he hadn't spoken to Ricky. He also knew that there was supposed to have been a tuxedo fitting.

"Why would I go all the way to Ricky's house if we were going to see each other at the fitting the next day?

Why didn't Toni try to talk me out of it? Was the fitting canceled? Toni didn't mention to me if it was or not. Fuck! That's why her ass needs to be here. Where the fuck is she?" he asked himself as he dialed her yet again.

The phone went straight to voice mail. Ty had a mind to call Maya. He figured she was over there anyway. He found it somewhat odd that she hadn't been over to check on him. That sure wasn't like her. Any other time, she'd be first in line for any drama, especially if he and Toni were involved.

"Come to think of it, Maya never even came to the hospital. Toni said that she never even heard from her. I swear this shit is strange, man!" Ty stated while shaking his head.

He grabbed the piece of paper off the coffee table and sat back in his recliner. He kept repeating over and over the same phrase. "I left work early to go to Ricky's house. I left work early to go to Ricky's house."

He finally dozed off but awoke in a cold sweat. His heart was racing, and his eyes were bulging out of his head. He dreamed that he was in a dark place. He could feel the place moving beneath him. *I dreamed I was in that trunk*, he thought.

He felt a sharp pain in his head and then experienced what seemed like a flashback of some sort. He saw himself pull up to Ricky's house, and he saw Steven's car in the driveway. *I made it to Ricky's house, but he wasn't alone*, he thought.

mwisho

An excerpt from *Appearances Too: Mask Off*

Maya ended up spending the night at her new house. Her condo seemed too empty without Ricky there. She woke up in a complete haze. She wanted to forget what had happened the night before. She wanted to forget what had happened, period, but she couldn't.

As hard as it was, she had to admit to her reality and decide what she was going to do to take control of the situation. She peeled herself off of the floor and began to put a plan together. *This house will have me and Steven in it when it's all said and done*, she thought.

80098203R00086

Made in the USA
San Bernardino, CA
22 June 2018